The
Haunted Ga

The Haunted Gathering

The Haunted Ones, Volume 4

Michelle Dorey

Published by Michelle Dorey, 2019.

THE HAUNTED GATHERING

First edition. October 19, 2019.

Copyright © 2019 Michelle Dorey.

ISBN: 979-8223907053

Written by Michelle Dorey.

Table of Contents

By
Michelle Dorey

About This Book

THE HAUNTED GATHERING

On their annual girls' weekend three friends gather for a macabre reunion in this chilling tale of ghosts, hauntings and the occult.

Dara died almost a year ago, and her three closest surviving friends gather in accordance with her last wishes at Gabbinger's Reach—a once abandoned resort she planned on restoring to opulence.

The derelict property has been decaying for decades. Cindy the career woman thinks this is stupid. Melanie, the flighty one is fascinated. Becky, now a therapist is curious—why would Dara want them here?

They're enticed to stay by Dara's Last Will and Testament. Each of them are promised riches, all they need to do is remain here for two nights.

When darkness descends on the first evening, they laugh off the sudden appearance of small gifts. They're only a little startled by things crashing around in the kitchen. Someone's trying to spook them; big freaking deal—Cindy brought a gun!

Their bravado is tested when they begin to uncover long held secrets. Secrets about each another, secrets about Dara, and long hidden secrets about the evil that infests the very walls of this place. Hungry evil relishing fresh victims.

At the same time their bonds of friendship are at the breaking point, the ravenous beast descends in a mighty fury. In a night of terror, they know they'll never be the same. If they survive.

Dara didn't.

Chapter ONE

REBECCA FINISHED TYPING THE LAST ENTRY into Bobbi Penstock's file. It had been a longer day than usual, cramming her schedule to clear up some time in September for the annual get-together. She clicked the mouse bringing up her personal email.

When Dara's email popped up, she smiled. *Finally,* there'd be some details of where they'd meet. Trust Dara to leave everything to the last minute, just like in college. Some things never changed.

TO: BECKY, MELANIE, CINDY
DATE: MONDAY, JUNE 28 AT 10:43 PM
SUBJECT: OUR 7TH ANNUAL REUNION BASH
HI LADIES,
SEVEN YEARS SINCE CALTECH! WHAT THE HELL? EVEN CRAZIER IS THE FACT THAT I ACTUALLY MISS THAT PLACE...SOMETIMES.
I KNOW YOU'RE ON THE EDGE OF YOUR SEATS WAITING FOR DETAILS OF OUR GET-TOGETHER (OR AS MELANIE CALLS IT "THE GATHERING") AT LEAST I HOPE YOU ARE SITTING DOWN BECAUSE...
I'VE GOT SUPER FANTASTIC PLANS FOR OUR REUNION THIS YEAR.
I BOUGHT A FREAKING RESORT!
THAT'S RIGHT. DARA ZUCKERMAN IS NOW THE OFFICIAL OWNER OF GABBINGER'S REACH, IN THE CATSKILL MOUNTAINS.
AND BEFORE YOU SUGGEST I SIGN UP FOR A FEW SESSIONS OF PSYCHO-THERAPY WITH YOU, BECKY, IT WAS THE DEAL OF A LIFETIME. TOO GOOD TO PASS UP! ROCK-BOTTOM STICKER PRICE.
I DON'T KNOW HOW MUCH YOU KNOW ABOUT THE BORSCH BELT IN THE CATSKILLS, BUT IN ITS HEYDAY

(1950S AND 60S) IT WAS THE PLACE FOR RICH NEW YORK JEWISH FOLKS TO GET AWAY FROM THE HEAT OF THE CITY TO RELAX. I'M NOT GOING TO GO INTO THE ANTI-SEMITISM THAT WAS RAMPANT DURING THAT TIME IN NYC, (WHICH, THANK GOD HAS CHANGED), BUT THE POPULARITY OF THE AREA FELL OFF DURING THE 70S AND 80S.

LIKE OTHER RESORTS, GABBINGER'S HAS BEEN ABANDONED FOR DECADES! SURE, IT NEEDS WORK AND MONEY, OF WHICH I'VE GOT TONS. THANKS DADDY, FOR THAT AT LEAST. (SIGH)

YOU'RE GOING TO LOVE IT, MELANIE, WITH THE SCENIC MOUNTAINS AND THE LAKE PRACTICALLY AT OUR FRONT DOOR. WHO KNOWS WITH THESE BUFF CONSTRUCTION GUYS, YOU MAY EVEN FINALLY GET A BOYFRIEND. GOT TO PUT YOURSELF OUT THERE A BIT, MEL. PUT DOWN THE CRYSTALS, TAROT CARDS AND BOOKS AND JOIN THE LIVING INSTEAD OF THE DEAD. YOU MIGHT LIKE IT. (TEASING OF COURSE. YOU KNOW I LOVE YOU JUST THE WAY YOU ARE.)

DON'T WORRY ABOUT HOW RUSTIC AND PRIMITIVE IT IS, CINDY. BY SEPTEMBER, OUR ACCOMMODATIONS WILL BE TOTALLY REVAMPED WITH EVERY CONVENIENCE YOU'D EVER WANT.

(AFTER WHAT HAPPENED IN CHICAGO, I OWE YOU THAT MUCH AT LEAST, ALTHOUGH I KNOW I WAS RIGHT DOING IT. ALL FORGIVEN? IF NOT, WE CAN COUNT ON BECKY TO "THERAPY" US, JUST LIKE BACK IN THE GOOD OLD DAYS SHARING THAT HOUSE ON CAMPUS. REMEMBER THE ICE-CREAM INCIDENT? THAT COULD HAVE GOTTEN REAL UGLY IF NOT FOR BECKY.)

BECKY, GIVE MY REGARDS TO HANK. HE'S GONNA HAVE TO COOK FOR HIMSELF WHILE YOU'RE GONE BUT BOO HOO. LOL

I KNOW THIS IS A FAR STRETCH FROM THE GLITZY VEGAS TRIP, CINDY. OR TRAIPSING OVER MAYAN RUINS, MELANIE...OR EVEN THE SEASIDE RESORT IN ROCKPORT, BECKY... BUT IT'S MY TURN TO CHOOSE THE VENUE THIS YEAR.

MY TURN, MY RESORT. SO THERE. SUCK IT UP, BUTTERCUPS.

BESIDES WHICH, I'M DYING TO SHOW IT TO YOU, MY OLDEST AND DEAREST FRIENDS! WELL...MAYBE NOT AS IT IS TODAY BUT WHAT I'M GOING TO DO WITH IT!

DID I MENTION THAT THE AREA IS UNDER CONSIDERATION BY THE STATE FOR MORE CASINO EXPANSION? THAT'S WHERE THE REAL MONEY IS. WELL THAT'S ONE AVENUE THAT MAKES THIS WORTHWHILE, BUT I'VE GOT SOME OTHER IDEAS TOO. HOW ABOUT AN ADULTS ONLY SPA? I DON'T CARE AS LONG AS THEY HAVE FULL POCKETS FOR ME TO PLUNDER. HOPEFULLY YOU'LL COME UP WITH MORE IDEAS!

I'VE HAD A CREW UP THERE FOR A MONTH WORKING. THERE'S A SECTION OF THE RESORT THAT'S ONCE MORE HABITABLE FOR US. DON'T WORRY, I'M GOING THERE TOMORROW TO CRACK THE WHIP AND MAKE SURE OF IT.

I'M ATTACHING A FEW PICS OF THE AREA AS WELL AS A MAP. NOT SURE THE GOOGLE CAR EVER MADE IT THIS FAR INTO THE BOONIES.

BESTIES FOREVER,

DARA

Rebecca sank back in the leather chair and exhaled slowly. Dara bought a resort in the Catskills? With the death of her father last year, she now had total control of the estate, so why not? Still, maybe she was biting off more than she could chew. Delayed grief reaction? Trying hard to relive her father's dreams? But she had made a tidy profit when she'd sold that art gallery two years ago.

The intercom on her desk buzzed bringing her out of the reverie. "Yes?"

"Your eleven o'clock is here. Shall I send him in?" Gloria's low voice let her know that Jason Knox was probably perched on the edge of the chair in the waiting room. No doubt his knee was twitching, looking forward to unloading the slights and injustices he'd suffered at the hands of his domineering mother the past week. No matter that he was thirty-four and still living under his parents' roof with zero job prospects.

"Give me five, Gloria. I'm just finishing up an article." No need to tell her receptionist she was still pondering Dara's email.

What was that *Chicago* thing all about? Something happened there between Dara and Cindy? Maybe she'd give Cindy a call later to get the dirt. Probably Dara had done something thoughtless. Tact and diplomacy weren't her strong suits, whereas Cindy was people-smart. She had to be to make it in that cutthroat business.

Rebecca turned slightly to gaze out the window at the expanse of chrome and mirrored buildings. If she leaned closer there was even a partial view of the Olympic Mountains, maybe if it wasn't hazy and overcast. Prime office space in downtown Seattle. Not bad for a kid who grew up in neighboring Tacoma. Like Melanie and Cindy, she'd had to work two jobs in the summer to pay for tuition. Even so, she was still paying off her student loans.

Dara. How they'd ever hooked up with a trust-fund kid and became friends was still a wonder. But to give Dara credit, she *was* fun to hang with. There was never a dull moment with her antics. Maybe she'd finally found her place in life with this abandoned resort, breathing life into it.

She pushed the button on her desk signaling that she was ready for Jason Knox. She'd answer the email after his session.

Never knowing that by that time, Dara would be dead.

Chapter TWO

That September...

"YOU DIDN'T MAKE HER *FUNERAL,* **CINDY.** This is the least that you can do!" Holding the phone in a death grip, Rebecca gritted her teeth so hard they clicked. It was bad enough that Cindy refused to tell her about the altercation she'd had with Dara in Chicago, but here she was trying to dodge the last request that Dara would ever make!

"Come on, Beck! Don't try to guilt me into going. As for the funeral, I was in *Australia,* for Pete's sake! Even if I decided to risk losing our biggest client and come back, I still couldn't have made it in time." The exasperation in Cindy's voice bordered on being whiny.

"Look. All I'm saying is that it's the last thing we'll ever get to do for Dara. And what about Melanie? You know how close to Dara she is...or rather was. This will totally devastate her if we all don't show up at this Gabbinger's place. *She* needs our support if nothing else." Rebecca's eyes narrowed. Whatever had happened between Cindy and Dara had to be pretty rough if she was so willing to skip out on the dead woman's last request.

Cindy's tone softened, "Poor Mel. But it's just so morbid. I mean Dara drowned there. And that thing in her will is creepy as hell. Who makes a will before they're even thirty, anyway?"

"I know. I wondered about that too. Was she depressed? Why would she go swimming at night, *alone?*" It wasn't the first time that she wondered if Dara had been suicidal. But she hadn't talked to Dara in months. Not something she was proud of, but people have their own lives. They get busy.

"That was so *Dara.* Invincible. She paid the ultimate price for her recklessness." There was silence for a few beats, both of them picturing their friend. "Have you spoken to Melanie? I mean since the funeral."

"I texted her a few times, and when she didn't answer I finally called. She's adamant that we all go there, to honor Dara's wishes. She... Well, you'll see for yourself anyway, but...she's gotten even more obsessed with this spiritualism shit."

"Of course, she has. She'll never change." Cindy's tone went from wistful to annoyed in the next breath. "That letter we all got from her lawyer...It wouldn't have killed him to give us more information to go on. Just be at Gabbinger's September twenty-first at four p.m. to honor Dara's last wishes. And we have to stay the weekend?"

Becky's voice hitched when she spoke. "Of course, you know that Dara's birthday is September twenty-second. She would have been twenty-eight. Way too young to die."

"You think she left us anything in the will?"

"Cindy! Is that all you're—"

"NO!" Her voice became softer after Becky's chastisement. "Just wondering is all. None of us need it. Well...maybe Mel could use it. But money was never Melanie's thing, right? Give her a book about goblins and poltergeists, and she's lost in her own world."

"She's not as strong as the rest of us, Cindy. That sort of stuff is her crutch—escaping into make-believe. That way she doesn't have to risk real relationships. I don't think she's made any friends since us back in university. She needs us, Cindy. Say you'll come. It's only forty-eight hours. Surely you can put your career on hold for that long."

A long sigh followed, and Becky's head rose higher. When Cindy mumbled a soft, "I guess," her eyes closed with relief.

She decided to press ahead before Cindy had a chance to change her mind. "My flight arrives in Newark at one ten. Mel's getting there at noon. I've booked a car for us. You're welcome to drive with us."

"How far is it from the airport?" Cindy's voice drooped with resignation.

"Two hours. Seriously, we might even manage to have fun, you know. I'm bringing wine. We can count on Mel for weed. We'll celebrate Dara's birthday as if she were there." Becky tried to sound upbeat, barely pulling it off. Yes. Cindy was right. This was downright weirdly morbid.

Still, it would be good to see Mel and Cindy. But the reunion bash with just the three of them, where Dara had actually died, was going to be sad.

To say the least. Partying at the spot where one of your best friends died? She shuddered inwardly.

"Fine. I'll book the flight and see you tomorrow. This place better have a damn bathroom! I'm not using some outhouse or something. And that lawyer, Anthony Wilson, better have it well stocked with food and drink."

"Thanks, Cindy. I also want to know what went down with you and Dara in Chicago."

"Don't push your luck, Becky." This was followed by a click.

Chapter THREE

BECKY GLANCED IN THE REAR-VIEW MIRROR watching Melanie speak, "I can't believe she's actually gone. I talked to her three nights before her death."

Melanie had lost weight and her skin which was normally pale now seemed translucent. With the wheat-blond hair hanging over her shoulders, she seemed even more frail and wraith-like.

Cindy pushed her sunglasses high on her head and turned slightly to answer her, "What did she say to you?"

"She told me she wanted me to do a smudging and use crystals to purify the resort." Melanie leaned forward resting her hand on the back of Becky's seat.

Becky didn't need to look at Cindy to know exactly what she was thinking. It was probably the same thought that had popped into her own head. Dara had been trying to placate Melanie, making the poor woman feel some sense of importance.

"That's it?" Cindy peered at Melanie, examining her face. "Did she seem off in some way? Swimming alone at night is crazy, even for Dara. She was alone, wasn't she? Did she say—"

"You mean *David*, don't you?" Melanie sat back, and a sly smile flitted across her face.

A quick glance at Cindy showed that Melanie had struck a nerve. Becky directed her question to Melanie before peering hard at the road again, "Who's David? I don't remember Dara ever mentioning him before. Was he her new flavor of the week?"

"Why don't you ask Cindy?" Melanie folded her arms over her stomach and gazed out the window. It was obvious that she knew the whole story about the 'thing' in Chicago.

A glance at Cindy showed her cheeks flaring a deeper shade of pink, and her chin had risen higher.

Cindy's words were clipped when she spoke. "David Gallagher. He was another promoter at the blues fest in Chicago. We dated a few times and hit it off right away. That was until Dara just happened to show up at our final evening of the tour. It was hard to say which she flaunted more—her cash or her ass. He left with her at the end of the night."

Melanie muttered from her seat in the rear, "Dara said he was a jerk. She knew all about him. A hanger-on looking for a meal ticket. She saw that you were falling for him. She dumped him right away, of course. Warned him to stay away from you, Cindy. So no, he wasn't at the resort that night she died."

Becky sneaked another glance at Cindy. "Did he ever contact you after that night?"

"No." Her voice was sullen.

They rounded a bend in the road, and the mechanical voice of the GPS interrupted, "In five hundred feet take the first right, onto Rider Lane."

Becky felt her ears pop. They had been steadily climbing higher in the mountains on a road that was becoming narrower, crowded on each side by dense evergreens with the odd colorful dash of yellow or orange fall foliage. Her foot eased from the gas pedal as she spied the small sign marking the side road.

"This really *is* remote, isn't it? The last town we passed was twenty minutes ago, and since then there's been only the odd house." Cindy gazed out the front windshield, her attention focused high in the hazy mountaintop. "We should be almost there by now. I mean it's been two hours on the road. I shouldn't have had that coffee on the plane."

Melanie's window slid down, and she poked her head out sniffing the clear air. "You can smell the pine and cedar in the air. There's something mystical about being in the mountains. I'm not surprised Dara chose this location." Her voice dropped, "Even if it is cursed."

Becky smiled, fumbling for anything other than going down Melanie's spiritual rabbit hole. "No glaciers here though. These mountains are small compared to the Cascades back home. But yes, it is beautiful. Still, I'm not sure that Dara was enchanted by any element aside from looking for a profit. She was a businesswoman to the bone."

Melanie edged forward once more, inserting herself between Cindy and Becky, "You're wrong about that, Becky. She and I were close. There was a side of Dara that she didn't show to many people. She had a dream one time about me getting hit by a car as I was crossing the street. She was so upset that she called me right away, the next morning."

Cindy snorted, "You're here in one piece, aren't you? You didn't get hit by any—"

"I *almost* did! A car ran a red light and missed me by mere inches! If I hadn't jerked back I would have been killed. Dara begged me to leave my cell phone at home when she called, and I *did*. In the dream, she saw me checking a text and not seeing the car zooming toward me. She probably saved my life that day."

"That sounds like a close call, for sure." Becky ignored the roll of Cindy's eyes. It could have been coincidence. Most likely thing...really.

When they rounded what seemed liked the hundredth bend in the road, Becky's foot jerked away from the gas pedal and she stiffened.

There it was. The resort where Dara had drowned. The first thing that drew her attention were twin rounded turrets, each one topped by a cone roof, green with verdigris. They hulked like sentries at each end of a three-story castle that sprawled out to an attached balcony overlooking an emerald-green lake.

"Oh my God." Melanie leaned forward peering up at the structure.

"It had better be nicer on the inside than out, if I'm staying here. I thought she had a crew doing renovations for a month. This is all they did? There're still broken windows on one side and vines are growing everywhere."

Becky forced her gaze away from the lake, looking to the side where two lower outbuildings hunkered. From the gaping hole where a garage door hung askew, she could see the back of a rusted tractor or lawn mower. The granite of several stone archways leading down overgrown paths were slick with moisture where the moss wasn't clinging. Everything was so still and quiet she could hear Melanie's breathing as she stared at the house.

When the front door of the building opened, her breath hitched in her throat. A tall man in a dark suit stepped out, eyeing them as he came down the wide set of stone steps. It was only then that she noticed a dark Escalade tucked off to the side of the curved drive.

"That's got to be the lawyer."

Becky drove the car into the spot behind him and paused before turning the key. It was probably her imagination, making her suddenly jittery. The place might be picturesque, but there was also a heavy feeling of foreboding about it. For the first time, her thoughts echoed Cindy's earlier misgivings—coming here was a morbid mistake.

She glanced at Cindy and Melanie. They felt it too from the silent pall that had fallen over them. This was real. This was Dara's final reunion with them. And far from what Dara had gushed about, the hotel didn't look all that welcoming.

Chapter FIVE

BECKY STEPPED OUT OF THE CAR watching the man come forward, his hand extended.

"I'm Anthony Wilson, Dara's lawyer. First of all, let me extend my deepest condolences to you...ah..."

She grasped his hand. "Rebecca Sloan." She turned slightly as Cindy stepped forward. "This is Cindy Evans." She signaled for Melanie to come closer. "This is Melanie Walker. Thank you for your sympathy."

He gave a long sigh, and his shoulders drooped lower. "I knew Dara for a long time. Her father was a client and friend." He paused for a moment and glanced over at the lake. "This whole business is...well, it's odd to say the least." A grim smile appeared on his face as he stepped back. "But we'll get into that later. Let me help you with your bags."

Cindy placed her hand on his arm. "Wait a minute on that, please. You've been inside, right? Is it really habitable? Bathrooms, kitchen...real beds, not cots?"

He snorted. "Of course. But I will warn you that it's only the one wing that's been completed. You'll find everything you need. Plus, it's only forty-eight hours." He took the bag that Melanie was pulling from the back seat and led the way across the broken pavement of the drive.

Cindy held back and whispered to Becky, "That guy must be loaded. His suit's easily ten grand. I swear it's beyond tailor-made, more like *bespoke* the way it fits. A few of my clients have suits like—"

Becky cut her off, rolling her eyes. "Seriously, Cindy? The guy's successful. So what? Remember why we're here, will you?" Shaking her head, she grabbed her bag from the trunk. Sometimes, Cindy could be so shallow, so easily impressed by successful guys flaunting their bank account on their back. She'd been hanging around too many flashy singers and bands.

"You're right. But truthfully, I'd rather think of her fancy lawyer than what happened here. This place gives me the heebie-jeebies. I need to break into that wine—and pronto." Cindy followed behind, tugging a wheeled suitcase that could have housed a small pony.

Becky stepped through the doorway, while the lawyer waved her through, a more serious expression on his long face. Her sneakered feet squeaked on the new oak floor in an open reception lit only by the sun's rays flooding through large windows above the door. Dara had kept the flavor of bygone days in selecting windows holding a grid of small panes. Aside from an immense chandelier hanging from exposed rafters two stories higher, an oak table and chairs in the center of the room were the only furnishings.

Melanie walked slowly over to the chair at the head of the table, sliding her fingertips along the high back. "This is probably where she worked, meeting with contractors and laying out plans. I can almost feel her sitting here." Her head turned and there was a wistful expression in her blue eyes.

Even Cindy managed to stay silent at Melanie's sadness, a fact that Becky was grateful for.

The lawyer walked over to the table and moved his briefcase to the other end, allowing Melanie to claim Dara's chair. He set it on the surface, and the click of the lock when it opened echoed in the still air. "I will show you your rooms and the facilities after we outline some provisions in Dara's will."

Becky's head snapped up from gazing at the far wall, the dust motes caught in the rays of the sun, to Anthony Wilson's face. From the looks of this, Dara may have included them in her estate. Cindy might have been correct in that assumption.

She followed Cindy and took a chair across from her, while Mr. Wilson set out a file folder. He placed the palms of his hand on top before opening it, looking at each one in turn. "As I said earlier, this whole thing is unusual. When Dara's father passed last year, leaving her his considerable estate, I urged Dara to draft a will, take care of things. She put me off, even after a few email reminders."

Becky sighed. "She needed time to grieve, Mr. Wilson. Her father was all she had, aside from an estranged uncle and some distant cousins." It was understandable that the lawyer's main concern was business but still, a little sensitivity could go a long way.

He cleared his throat and looked down at the file for a few beats. "Yes. Of course. But what was odd was that Dara came to me immediately after purchasing this property in order to set her affairs in order. But she was distraught at the time—not herself at all."

"She had some kind of dream, didn't she?" Melanie's voice was a whisper, her gaze impaling the lawyer like a skewer.

He actually jerked, and his lips parted slightly as he looked back at her. "Yes. How did you know? But of course, you were friends...?"

"Yes. But she never spoke of it when we talked." Melanie looked down at her hands clasped tightly, resting on the table's polished surface.

Cindy's auburn hair fell forward across her shoulders when she leaned forward. "What did she tell you?"

He sighed. "She said she'd had this dream of not being able to breathe—suffocating. It happened the day that reconstruction started on this resort. She linked the two things, but I assured her it was just nerves. She had planned to invest millions in this restoration. This was a project that she was hardly experienced in—tackling the renovations as well as lobbying the government for a casino expansion for this resort."

Melanie's voice was soft, her eyes gazing at the table, trance-like "She knew. She knew she was going to die here. Drowning is suffocation."

Becky stood up and went over to Melanie, stroking the woman's hair and squeezing her shoulder. "It's okay to cry, Melanie. We're all still grieving her loss. She was a good friend."

Cindy finally spoke, addressing the lawyer and breaking the silence. "Putting this dream or premonition aside, why are we here, Mr. Wilson? Believe me, I'd rather be drinking a toast to Dara in some superhot club rather than here at the place she died."

He nodded and opened the file folder, plucking a letter from it. "She wrote this and asked that I read it to you in the event of her death." He cleared his throat and began to read aloud:

"TO MELANIE, BECKY AND CINDY, MY BEST FRIENDS FOR ALL TIME. WITH THE DEATH OF MY FATHER LAST YEAR, I'VE BEEN SADLY REMINDED OF MY OWN MORTALITY. NOT THAT I PLAN ON CHECKING OUT ANYTIME SOON, BUT THIS IS THE 'RESPONSIBLE' THING TO DO, RIGHT?

"IT'S KIND OF SAD THAT THE CLOSEST BONDS I EVER MADE, ASIDE FROM MY DAD, WERE WITH YOU THREE. MY UNCLE IS AN ASS, AND HIS KIDS SWIM IN THE SAME GENE POOL. THE ONLY TIME I EVER FELT LOVED WAS BY YOU GALS. BELIEVE IT OR NOT, BUT OUR ANNUAL REUNION IS THE HIGH POINT OF MY YEAR.

"I AM LEAVING YOU MY ESTATE IN EQUAL SHARES. BUT I WANT ONE LAST TIME WITH YOU. ONE LAST CELEBRATION. ON MY FIRST BIRTHDAY AFTER I CHECK INTO THE BIG HOTEL IN THE SKY, I'D LIKE YOU TO GET TOGETHER, JUST LIKE WE HAVE ALWAYS DONE AT OUR REUNION BASHES. BUT, I'M COUNTING ON YOU GALS TO BE OLD LADIES BY THEN, TEETERING ON YOUR WALKERS, AS I DON'T PLAN ON GOING ANYWHERE ANYTIME SOON! LOL.

"BUT...SAD NOTE... DAD THOUGHT HE'D LIVE TILL HE WAS NINETY-NINE, AND HE DIED AT FIFTY-EIGHT.

"WEIRD NOTE NOW... I'VE BEEN HAVING HORRID DREAMS. SOMETHING OPPRESSIVE CLINGS TO ME AND

ONLY MAKES ITSELF KNOWN WHEN I FALL ASLEEP. IT STARTED WHEN THE RENOS BEGAN AT GABBINGER'S REACH. PERHAPS I WASN'T MEANT TO BUY IT...EVEN THOUGH I LOVE THE PLACE. I KNOW THAT CINDY AND BECKY WILL THINK I'M EITHER DOING CHEAP DRUGS OR THAT I'M IN SOME KIND OF PARANOID DEPRESSION. BUT MELANIE, I THINK YOU UNDERSTAND WHERE I'M COMING FROM.

"WITH THAT IN MIND, I NEED YOU LADIES. TOAST TO MY LIFE WITH YOU, MY BEST FRIENDS. GIVE ME A HAPPY SEND-OFF SO THAT I DON'T BECOME A LONELY SPIRIT, TRAPPED IN SOME CRAZY IN-BETWEEN PLACE.

"THIS IS ALL PREFACED WITH MY CONVICTION TO OUTLIVE YOU ALL. ESPECIALLY YOU, CINDY. REMEMBER WE WERE ALWAYS COMPETITORS. I'M JUST HEDGING MY BETS, IS ALL.

"I NEED YOU TO STAY WHEREVER I DIE FOR FORTY-EIGHT HOURS, CELEBRATING MY FIRST BIRTHDAY AFTER THAT HAPPENS. IT'S A SMALL THING TO ASK CONSIDERING OUR FRIENDSHIP AND THAT YOU ARE ALSO MY HEIRS. IF ANY OF YOU PREDECEASE ME OR ARE UNABLE TO COMPLY WITH THIS REQUEST, YOU FORFEIT YOUR PORTION OF THE MONEY I'M LEAVING YOU."

The lawyer looked up before setting the letter down. Before he had a chance to say another word, Cindy posed the question, "How much are we talking about, Mr. Wilson?"

Becky paused, her hand still on Melanie's shoulder. Even Melanie waited with expectant silence, her eyes narrowed.

"You would each inherit close to ten million dollars.

Chapter FIVE

"**TEN MILLION!**" Becky now clutched Melanie's shoulder in a death grip.

"Ow!" Melanie jerked away, rubbing herself. "That hurt!"

"Sorry." Becky patted the woman's shoulder. This was astounding! She'd known that Dara had money but thirty million?

Cindy raised her hand. "I'm in! I'll give Dara the send-off of a lifetime! Hell, I'll even forgive her for the whole David thing." Cindy grinned and did a fist pump to the universe. "Yes! No more irritating clients. I can open up my own company and hire people to put up with that shit!"

Melanie brushed her hand through the air, waving off Cindy's excitement. "Cindy! Dara needs us. She died here. She even had a premonition of her own death, enough so that she wrote that letter! I don't care about the money! I'd give everything I own just to hear Dara laugh again...to be able to talk to her."

The lawyer interjected before things got even more tense between Cindy and Melanie. "As Dara's executor, I need to ensure that you are here abiding by her last wishes. That means all of you. I will return in forty-eight hours with certified checks for each of you. If only two are here, then two of you will receive the estate funds equally. The additional money will be split between those two, or even given to one if that's the situation."

Becky took her seat again, asking as she settled into her chair, "If you have food and beverage on hand, we should be able to manage. We will honor Dara's wishes."

Cindy spoke. "Hang on. If we need something in town, maybe want to have lunch there or something? That's okay, right? As long as we're here—"

"No. You need to be here for the full forty-eight hours." The lawyer shook his head.

18

Becky stared at the lawyer. "What about medical emergencies? Surely if we *had* to leave for a short period, that would be okay? Provided of course we're here to meet you. In forty-eight hours."

"I will leave the number of the Liberty Ambulance Service. They are authorized with a stipend already supplied, to come here if you require them. All other transport, taxis, ride-sharing companies are under strict orders to stay away." He cleared his throat once more, sliding the folder back into his briefcase. "I will of course make note of the mileage on your vehicle before I leave."

This was beyond odd, bordering on what a prison sentence would be like. Mr. Wilson was completely anal retentive about complying with the exact terms of the will.

"Wow! You've covered all the bases, haven't you?" Cindy rose to her feet, wandering over to take the handle of her bag. "Please show us the rest of this creepy place, Mr. Wilson. You won't be able to pry me away from here with a crowbar for another forty-eight hours. Trust me."

Chapter SIX

THE LAWYER ROSE and started across the room to an archway. "If you'll follow me, I'll show you your rooms and the kitchen. I'm afraid the dining room renovations were never completed."

"Please make the first stop the bathroom. Too many coffees and too long a drive here." Cindy left everything behind, hustling to catch up with the middle-aged man. Unlike Becky and Melanie, she was dressed to impress, her four-inch stilettos clacking on the wood, her legs in the tight spandex working fast.

The lawyer suppressed a smile. "I'm sorry. I should have asked before we started if you needed to use the facilities." He walked briskly down the hallway and opened a door on the left. "This is the first bedroom. You'll find that, of course, with an attached bath."

Becky exchanged a look with Melanie as Cindy rushed inside the room. "I guess she's laying claim to that one." She stepped over the threshold, noting the wide picture window that overlooked broken paths, and gardens which were given over to vines and weeds, the land sloping down to the lake. The smell of fresh paint lingered faintly in the air above a massive, king-sized bed, the sides of the royal blue duvet skimming the surface of wide oak flooring.

Melanie's voice just behind her startled Becky. "If Cindy doesn't mind, I'd like to claim this room. It feels right to me. I think Dara chose this room for herself. Even the color of the spread is pure Dara."

The sound of the toilet flushing and water in the sink was followed by Cindy appearing in the frame of the bath's doorway: a smile of relief on her full lips. "Thank God. There's even a Jacuzzi tub in there. I wouldn't mind this room—"

"I'm claiming it, Cindy. There are probably Jacuzzis in the other rooms as well," Melanie interrupted in an assured tone. The only sign that this was something new to her, stating a preference rather than deferring to Cindy, were the two spots of pink that colored her ivory cheeks.

Becky shot a look at Cindy, signaling to leave this alone. It was just a room, and if Mel wanted it, so what?

Cindy shrugged. "Sure. No biggie." She joined the lawyer who was standing in the doorway watching silently. "Lead on, MacDuff. There'd better be a well-stocked wine cellar. Just kidding. I brought my own to be on the safe side."

He nodded. "Of course. But you will find an ample supply of wine and liquor. As I didn't know what you ladies preferred, I made sure there was a generous assortment." As he led them to the next room, he continued, "You're right that the rooms are furnished with the same amenities. The only one that lacks a view of the lake is the fourth on this floor. It overlooks the garden and somewhat overgrown tennis courts."

Immediately, Cindy replied, "That's the one for me, then!" She turned to face Becky who was trailing behind her. "Sorry, Becks, but I find the prospect of looking at that lake downright depressing. I'll take weed-choked gardens any day."

Typical Cindy. Looking out for number one, like always. Becky nodded and waited for Melanie to catch up.

It was beginning to look like it would be up to her to keep the others grounded. Yes, this stay was odd and morbid, no question about that. But with the two-nights' stay looming, dark lonely nights in the middle of nowhere, she couldn't let Melanie's superstitions and "feelings" become paramount, having any sort of negative influence on Cindy. They were lucky that Cindy had agreed to come at all.

But that ten mil had sure changed her tune.

Melanie touched her arm as they followed the lawyer. In a low voice she said, "I don't mind doing the cooking for all of us. It'll be a nice change from eating alone. I mean you can't really count my cat as company."

Becky turned and smiled at her. "How is Mr. Whiska? Who's looking after him?"

"My neighbor is dropping by a couple times, checking on him. Not that there's much to do. Cats are so independent."

"That's good," she replied, nodding. "Thanks for taking that chore over."

"Well, I am a better cook than you." Melanie pointed at the door to the room Cindy took. "And Cindy won't argue for the job, right?" she added with a snicker.

That was true. What Becky also thought was true was that giving Melanie something to look after while they were here wouldn't hurt. She was more preoccupied with Dara's death than either of the other two. Having steady chores three times a day would help keep her mind in the here and now.

The lawyer opened the door to the room next to Melanie's for Becky. "I guess you get this one by default. Well, either this or the next one in line. Dara had wanted the floor of this wing ready for your reunion."

Becky walked inside and looked around. It was identical to Melanie's except that the color scheme was in shades of green from the softness of mint to a dark forest hue. She plopped down on the bed testing its firmness. Perfect. But of course, that would be quite like Dara getting the top of the line in furniture.

"Great. I'm sure you're anxious to be on your way, Mr. Wilson, so maybe we should take a look at that kitchen." She rose to her feet and joined the others. "The resort is huge. I'd like to explore it a little tomorrow."

The lawyer clucked his tongue before looking at her. "Just be careful." He raised his eyes scanning their surroundings. "The building is sound for the most part but there may be floorboards which have given way to dry rot if they aren't actually ruined by the elements. The place has been abandoned for over thirty years."

Cindy chimed in, "So what happens to this place after this weekend? Will you try to sell it to recover some of the money she sunk into it?"

The lawyer stopped and looked at each of them in turn. "It will be abandoned. Eventually the local government will claim it for unpaid taxes. That was a final provision in Dara's will. Abandon it if it's not complete. An odd bit of foresight on her part."

Chapter SEVEN

THEY MADE THEIR WAY BACK to the reception area. Mr. Wilson left his business card on the table with the phone number for the ambulance service written on the back and made his goodbyes.

"Good luck to you all," he said. "I'll see you in forty-eight hours." And that was that.

Cindy picked up the card. "Boy, that guy covered all bases ensuring we stick with it, here." She set it down and grabbed the handle of her suitcase, following Becky and Melanie.

Melanie stopped before entering her room, hugging her small bag to her chest. "It's almost six o'clock. When do you want to eat? I thought I'd marinate those chicken breasts in the fridge with lemon juice. How about salad and rice with it?"

Cindy called over her shoulder as she entered her own room. "I'm having at least three glasses of wine before I eat. You can serve dinner anytime after that."

"Or you can eat warmed up leftovers! Maybe Becky and I are hungry! Ever think of that, Cindy?" Melanie's voice held an edge.

Becky stopped and looked over at Melanie. This was a side to her mousy friend which was entirely new. She'd always thought Melanie needed to be more assertive, and maybe Dara's death had brought that out. Dara had always been protective of Melanie—to a fault really. It hadn't helped Mel's personal growth, and now that she was gone, well, good for Melanie.

Becky raised her voice a little so that Cindy would hear. "How about seven? I'd like to check out the grounds, stretch my legs after the flight and long car ride. You can come along and bring your wine." She caught Melanie's eye and winked. "And for God's sake, change into jeans and sneakers, will you? This is wilderness not a fashion runway, Cindy. It's just us girls now."

Melanie shot Becky a grin and then darted into her room.

As Becky stepped into her own room and started to unpack, she realized that she had fallen into the same pattern of behavior: negotiator, keeping the peace. She placed her clothes in the dresser and then ran her fingers through her hair, glancing in the mirror at her reflection. A sweet-smelling, nutmeg-like scent drifted into her nostrils. Reflexively, she sniffed at her fingers wondering if it was the smell of her shampoo that she sensed. No, that wasn't it.

Another glimpse in the mirror showed a sprig of white flowers and dark waxy leaves resting on the mossy green comforter on the bed. She turned and walked over to it, staring down at the cluster of flowers. Jasmine. That was the scent she had picked up.

Her eyebrows knit together trying to recall if the flowers had been there when she sat on the bed earlier. She would have smelled it even if she didn't see it. It's a strong, sweet scent that can be overpowering sometimes.

No. It hadn't been there before. They'd been together with the lawyer except for Cindy's bathroom break.

"Becky!" The clack of Cindy's footsteps followed her voice.

When she appeared in the doorway of the room, her hand was outstretched, clutching the stem of a single yellow rose. "How did this get on my pillow?" Her dark eyes widened so that the white rims showed around them. "You got flowers too?"

Melanie stepped in next to her. In her hand was a bloom of lilac. "Me too! I swear I didn't put that there, and I know it wasn't there earlier either." Her voice dropped to a whisper. "It was Dara! These flowers. Each one is our personal favorite. Remember? She always gave a bouquet of jasmine to you Beck, yellow roses to you Cindy, and of course, I don't know how she managed to get them in February, but I always got lilacs on my birthday."

Becky stood up and grasped the sprig of jasmine, sniffing it. How the heck... Her jaw tightened. "There's got to be a logical explanation for this. Which means we really *do* have to explore the grounds. We're not alone in this resort. Somehow, Mr. Wilson has arranged for someone else to be here, planting these flowers while we were outside saying goodbye to him."

Cindy nodded. "Huh. How do we know that he isn't the one to get all that cash if we leave here early? We didn't see the entire will. We just know what he read to us and told us. Five will get you ten that he pockets the cash if we leave."

Melanie wasn't convinced. She shook her head slowly. "No. It was Dara. It's her way of welcoming us. She's here. I know it."

Chapter EIGHT

ANTHONY WILSON FLIPPED OPEN the top button of his shirt and tugged at his tie. A glance in the rear-view mirror before he rounded the bend, leaving Gabbinger's Reach behind, showed only the women's rental car parked in the circular drive. Already, they'd gone back inside to begin this...this macabre reunion that Dara had cooked up.

His stomach roiled, and he was forced to the side of the road, barely getting the door open in time before the lunch he'd had earlier, spewed forth onto the shoulder. His forehead was damp with sweat despite the coolness of the day, the sun now setting.

He'd been able to hold it together, hiding behind the professional shield in the short visit with those friends of Dara's. But now, safely on his way, the queasiness he'd felt when he stepped onto the property claimed his body in wracking heaves.

The whole business with Dara was beyond weird. He grabbed a tissue from the glove box and wiped his mouth, all the while recalling how frantic she'd been to get the will drafted. Doreen had tried to reschedule Dara's appointment, moving it ahead, but still she'd insisted that she had to meet with him that very day. When she arrived, she'd already had her will written with the letter attached as a codicil. She'd calmed down enough during that appointment that he'd been assured of her soundness of mind but now he wasn't so sure.

Was the drowning a successful suicide attempt? But that made no sense. Not from what she'd written in her letter. She planned on outliving them all or at least live to a ripe old age. And buying the resort, renovating it with big plans for its revival didn't jive with plans to end your life.

But there was something about that place. He'd felt it in the tiny hairs at the back of his neck when he'd stepped out of the car. The one woman, Melanie, had felt it too. Something was definitely off about the place, from the vibes that he'd picked up. Sure, some of that could be chalked up to the fact that a client, who was also a friend, had drowned there, but it was more than that.

He got back inside the car and sat for a moment silently. He could go back there and warn them to keep their guard up, pay attention and stay together at all times. Hell, maybe he could even look the other way if they decided to leave and still give them their share of the estate. If they were *his daughters,* he wouldn't feel easy about leaving them stranded in that resort. What if something happened to them?

He'd love to be able to write these superstitious feelings off! A year ago, he would have without a second thought.

But...

After that encounter with that kid, Adam Rafferty, all that changed. Adam had some very strange things happen to him, all the while claiming that he was being stalked by some other-worldly entity. It had been touch-and-go defending him during the police interrogation when some heavy circumstantial evidence pointed directly at the poor kid. He would have dismissed the kid as a nutcase except for the fact that *both* Mike Drogan, a retired detective, *and* the other guy, Jake, a freaking former FBI agent vouched for him! On top of that, he experienced Adam's gifts firsthand. The kid was tuned into another realm, able to *know* people's deepest darkest secrets.

Anthony sighed. No, he couldn't discredit his gut feeling. There was something bad in that damn resort. And not necessarily of this world.

He gave his head a sharp shake. "Jesus!" he said out loud. He was a goddamn lawyer! Not some crystal rubbing, incense burning New Ager! He'd spent his life practicing the law with a fiduciary responsibility to his client, even though she was deceased. He was a professional with all the trappings of the law to adhere to. He couldn't violate the terms of the will with a clear conscience.

Still.

"Oh for Chrissakes!" He pulled out his cell phone and hit a number in his contact list. It rang for a few rings before the tired voice of the detective answered.

"Mike Drogan Investigations."

"Mike. It's Anthony Wilson. I've got a bit of a situation I'm dealing with and could use your help." Anthony clutched the phone's receiver tightly, his other hand wiping a bead of sweat from his temple. Shit, his stomach was roiling again.

"Where are you?"

"I'm in the Catskills, just outside the town of Liberty." He huffed a breath. "It's about a four-hour drive from your place."

"What's up? What do you want me to do?"

"Surveillance. At least that's all I hope I'll need you for." He took a deep breath, and trying to keep his voice steady, said, "Mike...it's an odd situation."

"Odd, huh?"

"Yes."

After a few beats of silence, Mike spoke. "Tell you what, I'll throw some things in a bag and let Hilda know I'm going to be away for... How long do you need me for?" Mike's voice had perked up.

"Forty-eight hours. I need you to lie low, but keep an eye on an old resort where some women are staying. Ever hear of Gabbinger's? That's the place. It belongs to a deceased client, and her last wishes were for her gal pals to spend forty-eight hours there. But there's something off about this thing. I don't get a good feeling about them being there."

Anthony already felt a bit better enlisting the old detective's help. There'd be no way in God's green earth he'd ever admit to having this sense of foreboding to anyone but Mike. They had a history.

"By 'something off,' I take it you mean the resort, not the women." He sighed and then his voice lowered. "You want me to get Adam in on this? You know...well, he could be of some use. They give them a break at the academy over the weekend. He kind of owes both of us."

Of course, Mike was right. If he was totally honest with himself that was half the reason he'd called. Mike could keep the resort under surveillance to a certain extent, but Adam...well, if there was something foul and spooky about the place, he'd know what it was at a glance.

"Sure. If he can make it. And Mike, considering how last minute this is, your fee will be doubled. Call me when you get close to Liberty. I got a hotel room there."

"Okay. I should be there by ten or so."

"Mike? Make sure you bring the kid."

"Got it."

Anthony clicked the phone off and then put the car in gear. He'd done as much as he could for these women while still managing to adhere to the terms of Dara's will. Thank God all of this would be a mere memory in forty-eight hours.

He hoped. Oh God, how he hoped.

Chapter NINE

EACH OF THEM LOOKED AT THEIR FLOWERS SILENTLY.

Becky shared a skeptical look with Cindy when Melanie repeated, this time louder, "It's GOT to be Dara! She's here! Don't you feel her presence?"

Cindy placed her hand on Melanie's arm. "No, Melanie. Dara is dead. Gone. No lingering spirit, no essence or whatever you call it. Don't get me wrong. I miss her. I can't even look at that damn lake where she drowned." Her voice became firm, "There's some other person here with us. Becky's right. We need to check the place over."

Melanie shook Cindy's hand off, "Wait. You think the lawyer is somehow behind this? He said he put in an assortment of liquor, including scotch which we all hate. Yet you think Dara went to the trouble of telling her freaking lawyer what our favorite flowers are? I'm not buying that one."

Becky went over to Melanie and grasped her hands, rubbing the backs with her thumbs. "Melanie, I know this is hard. Especially being here where Dara's life ended. But we need to check this place out. Do you really want to sleep here knowing there might be someone else lurking around? If we see any evidence that someone else is here, we call that lawyer and find out what his game is."

Cindy eased away from them, returning to her room. "Give me five, Becky. I'll get changed into jeans and sneakers. The wine can wait."

Melanie lifted the spray of lilacs to her nose and inhaled. "You'll see. She's here. I know it." She turned and walked back to her room.

"Are you going to help us search the place, Melanie?" But Becky didn't hold out much hope on that score.

"Nope. I'll be in the kitchen. Lemon chicken was one of Dara's favorite dishes." The door to her room closed with a click of the latch.

Becky went back into her room and tossed the jasmine into the wastebasket. What would they do if they did find someone lurking around?

At the sound of Cindy's door closing, she turned to face her. The woman was sure a quick-change artist, her hair pulled up in a ponytail, wearing a Caltech sweatshirt and jeans. When her hand rose, there was a black pistol in it.

Becky's eyes widened. "What the hell? Since when did you start toting a gun around?"

"Since I dated a cop for a few months last year. He urged me to get one and even taught me to shoot straight. I'm out late many nights in my business. I've encountered more than a few sketchy characters when I've left a club or a booking. This nine Glock is a real confidence booster." Cindy gave the dark weapon a fond glance and then held it at her side, pointed down.

"All right. In that case, I won't need to stop by the kitchen to grab a cleaver." Becky shook her head but was glad that they weren't entirely defenseless at the remote lodge. "So what happened with the cop?"

Cindy shrugged. "Bill was nice and all but our schedules didn't work well together. Plus, I think he was looking for a wife. There's no way I'd marry a cop, never knowing when he went out the door, whether he'd be coming back."

Becky fell into step beside her walking down the hall to check out the final room in the wing of the hotel. "Yeah. Their life expectancy is pretty short. It's dangerous being a cop in Chicago."

Cindy nudged her with her shoulder. "There's more to us breaking up than that. Do you know how many of those guys screw around on their wives? 'The blue chick magnet' was how Bill described the uniform. No. When I marry it'll be for keeps." She grinned and then pushed the door to the vacant fourth bedroom open.

Becky followed Cindy who was looking all *Dirty Harry* holding the gun before her in a two-handed grip. This room was lavender colored, from the walls to the giant bed tucked up against the far wall. Her hand gripped Cindy's shoulder stopping her as the woman started to open a closet door.

On the pillow of the bed was a red rose. Becky's heart beat faster and she swallowed hard. Red roses were Dara's favorite flower. Oh God. There had to be someone here. This was a set-up.

Cindy gritted her teeth, tugging the closet door open and immediately resumed her threatening stance with the gun. She shook her head seeing only a few wooden hangers swaying in the small space.

"Is anyone here?" Becky forced authority into her voice, looking at the bathroom door which was ajar slightly. "Come out if you're in there."

But Cindy wasn't expecting compliance. She brushed by Becky and kicked at the door, stepping in and yanking the shower curtain back after seeing only the toilet and large vanity. If Cindy was scared, she sure didn't look it from the way she moved with catlike stealth.

"Are you two having fun?"

Becky jerked back, holding her hand over the hard skip in her chest. She let out a breath seeing Melanie standing in the doorway. "Shit, Mel! You scared the hell out of me!"

But Melanie was tearing across the room to the bed, scooping up the red rose. "Oh my God. We're complete now! She's here!" Her face lit up looking around the room like she'd seen the second coming of Christ.

"It's a rose. So what? Probably planted by the same jerk who put the flowers in our rooms." Cindy held the gun at her side again, skimming by Melanie. "I'd suggest you stay by our sides, Mel, until we find this guy...or guys."

But Melanie held the rose to her face, sinking down onto the bed instead. Cindy signaled for Becky to follow her, leaving the blond wraith alone with her memories of Dara.

Cindy whispered when they were out in the hallway. "She's losing it, Becky. I'm not even a shrink and I can see that. How is she going to handle forty-eight hours here?"

Becky forced a wan smile. "Forty-six now, to be exact. She's harmless, Cindy. Let her be. Once we find out whoever left those flowers she'll snap to. You'll see."

They passed by the other rooms and opened a door that they hadn't noticed before when the lawyer took them through. It opened to a set of stairs leading to the next floor. Unlike the hallway and rooms they'd just left, this area was strewn with cobwebs fluttering in the breeze from the open door. Light from a narrow window on the level above showed an iron staircase, rusted and hanging slightly askew. Dampness still clung to the old plaster walls, staining it in several areas with dark mold.

"Looks like the renos hadn't gotten as far as the floors above. Think those stairs are safe?" Becky stepped forward testing the first stair with her foot, bouncing a little to see if the supports moved at all.

"They look solid enough, just rusty is all. You better go first though. You're at least twenty pounds lighter than me." Cindy's eyes were wide eyeing the staircase and trying to see to the floor above.

Becky sneered and rolled her eyes casting a glance back at her friend. "Great. Being five-foot nothing, I was always envious of you and Dara...your height. Once more I regret inheriting my mother's genes."

A loud crash sounded from the floor above them. Becky's foot felt the impact on the stairs and she jerked back. She stared at Cindy, managing to get out a whisper from her mouth which had suddenly dried up. "What was that?"

Cindy snorted. "The floral delivery guy, who else?" But her hands holding the gun higher trembled a little.

Becky stepped back closer to the door. "You'd better lead the way. You've got the gun at least." Who knew what kind of thug might await them on the next level? Rickety rusty stairs were the least of their problems. Her heart hammered fast in her chest.

Cindy held the gun higher, grabbing the rail of the stairs as she tiptoed up. Becky followed a couple of steps behind, her gaze darting farther up the staircase to the landing and door above, tensed for confrontation with some thug.

A loud creak of straining metal rang through the air when Cindy took the next stair. The sound shot an arrow of fear straight through Becky's chest. Whoever was up there *had* to have heard that! He was bound to come flying down to attack them at any minute. The element of surprise was now shattered.

"Hurry, Cindy! We've got to get off these stairs."

Cindy cast a quick look back at Becky before taking the final two stairs in one leap. She pushed at the door and resumed her two-handed grip on the gun, holding it out. "I know you're up here. I'm armed. Show yourself." Her voice boomed, echoing back and bouncing in the air.

Becky glanced up at the stairs leading to the floor above them. There was no way anyone was going up there. The stairs hung precariously in the small chamber, leaving a gap of five feet between where she stood on the landing and where the stairs began.

She followed Cindy into the second-floor area. The space was so silent and still that Becky could hear her heartbeat thundering in her ears. Looking past Cindy's arms, she saw a dim hallway, littered with paper and broken furniture. The walls, aside from the gaping holes in places, were marred with graffiti. Even though a few of the doors tilted, clinging to the frame with just one hinge, it looked like a similar layout to the main floor below.

Shit! They'd have to go through every room to find the sneaky bastard.

Cindy turned and whispered loudly, "You stay here. Yell if anyone comes out of those rooms. That stairwell is their only means of escape."

Becky's hands rubbed at her upper arms protectively. "No way. I'm sticking to you like glue. You've got the gun." She sidled closer to her friend, shadowing her into the first room.

Light from a window illuminated the center of the room, the floor littered with tufts of grayish stuffing from a mattress propped up against one wall. A dark wooden dresser lay on its side, empty of drawers. A metal bed frame lay in twisted pieces closest to the nearest wall. Aside from these broken artifacts of a bygone era there was nothing else to show what had caused the loud crash they'd heard earlier.

She followed Cindy to the bathroom where a vanity held a blackened sink. Becky's nostrils pinched tight seeing the dark mold and mildew slinking up the walls above, almost to the ceiling. She'd be lucky if she didn't get sick after being in the filthy room. Again, the toilet and tub were stained and smudged with a substance she didn't even want to know about.

Cindy turned to her, and her voice was a low hiss. "Pretty yucky. I guess this place has seen its share of vandals over the years. Dara sure had her work cut out restoring this place."

"Let's check the next room." She waited for Cindy to lead the way out, trying not to touch anything.

Again, litter filled almost the whole floor while some wannabe artist had drawn crude pictures in red and black markers. There was everything from pentagrams to hearts and explicit depictions of both sexes' genitalia. But there was nothing that could have produced the loud banging noise.

The sound of a creaking board coming from farther along in the wing of the building made Becky freeze. She gripped Cindy's arm in a death clutch. "There's someone in the other room. What if they're armed too?"

Cindy shook her head. "The lawyer set it up to scare us, not kill us." She shrugged her arm away and continued, storming out of the room like a commando raider. "We know you're up here. Come out now with your hands in the air where I can see them!"

Becky peeked out the doorway watching Cindy disappear into the room across the hall. Her heart was going ninety miles an hour. She was ready to bolt for the stairwell at the slightest sound.

"Cindy? You okay? Talk to me, Goose." There was no reply.

She darted over to the room where Cindy was. Immediately she noticed torn curtains at a broken window fluttering in the breeze. A massive, broken armoire lay under it, which Cindy was squeezing by, trying to peer out the window.

When Becky neared her friend she could see the cedar shakes of a roof below, probably the kitchen area on the main floor. "You think whoever was up here escaped out the window?"

Cindy nodded. "That's the only explanation. Maybe in their hurry to get out of here, they accidentally knocked this hunk of junk over. That was the loud noise. But we'd better check the last room just to be on the safe side."

Becky nodded and edged back, almost tripping over a wooden box that she hadn't noticed before. Cindy strode by her and out the door to check the last room. The sound of Cindy moving fast, kicking the door open and checking the room followed.

If Cindy was right, they should go back down. Maybe Melanie had heard the intruder landing on the kitchen's roof.

But it still didn't explain the creaking floorboard that she and Cindy had heard, way after the intruder would have leapt out the window.

This place was creepy enough on its own, without someone planted there to frighten them.

Chapter TEN

BECKY SHUDDERED, brushing cobwebs from her sweater and hair as she followed Cindy from the stairwell. It wasn't just the insects and refuse in the ancient rooms above that crawled over her skin like lice. The place was damp and cold, even though the temperature outside was still in the mid-sixty range.

When they crossed the main reception area, Melanie was just coming out of the kitchen door at the far end. Becky noticed that Melanie seemed calm, even humming a song as she emerged from the doorway.

"Did you see or hear anything Mel? A noise above you or—"

"No. Why? Was I supposed to?" She tucked a stray lock of hair behind her ear, peering at Cindy and Becky like they were speaking Greek.

Cindy sighed and shook her head. "We think whoever was up on the second floor jumped down onto the kitchen's roof to escape." She looked around the reception area. "He could be anywhere by now. There're two other wings to this place, plus some outbuilding where he could be hiding."

Melanie chimed in, her voice wistful and with a singsong tinge. "Orrrrr...you could just accept the fact that Dara is making her presence known."

Becky ignored Mel's comment. Her shoulders slumped. It was bad enough that they had to spend two nights here, but now there was some kind of intruder trying to scare them. Cindy was right. They weren't cut out to confront some thug. That lawyer was up to something, and if he wasn't, then he sure as hell needed to know the danger he'd put them in. Surely getting some security or the police to check this place out wouldn't be breaking any of the will's provisions.

She went over to the long table where he'd left his business card. The table was empty, only the last gleam of sunshine splayed on its dark surface. "Where's that guy's card? You were the last person to handle it, Cindy. Give it to me, so I can call him and get someone out here...the police, if we need to."

Cindy looked at her blankly. "I left it on the table, so we'd know where it was in case we needed it." She turned her attention to Melanie who was standing with her arms folded across her chest, her gaze flitting between both her friends.

"What? I didn't take it, if that's what you think. I was in the kitchen getting things ready for dinner. Someone has to look after getting a meal together." Her face was the picture of innocence, staring wide-eyed.

Becky looked over at Cindy. She was the one who'd insisted that nothing was going to pry her away from her chance to get ten million dollars. She was also the only one who'd thought to bring a gun with her—an odd choice that put her at a distinct advantage. Who knew what lengths she'd go to, to get her hands on that money? Becky had firsthand knowledge from her therapy practice of what greed could do to a person.

Becky smiled at her friend to soften her words. "Are you sure you didn't unconsciously slip it in your pocket? I've been known to do stuff like that. Putting something away for safekeeping and then forgetting where I chose to stash it. Hank's always teasing me about it. My 'senior moments' he calls it."

"No! Look, if you don't believe me, you can check my things." She shoved her hands in her pockets and pulled the pocket lining out for Becky to see. "Nada. And my yoga pants don't have pockets. I'd remember if I took that card, trust me."

Melanie wandered closer to her friends, "Are you two going to continue your Nancy Drew shtick, or can we sit down and enjoy a glass of wine together? There's a cold bottle of Riesling in the fridge. We should begin with a toast to our hostess."

Cindy looked over at Becky, rolling her eyes. "I just need to know that we can lock our bedrooms, and no one will be able to get in here during the night. If that guy is out there, he's not getting back in. Is there a door to the outside in the kitchen? I never noticed one earlier, Mel." She was already on her way to check it, not trusting whatever would come out of Melanie's mouth.

In the meantime, Becky strode over to the front door, checking the lock and then double checking it again before she walked across the room to join her friends in the kitchen.

Melanie had four wineglasses set on the stainless-steel counter, pouring wine into each of them. Cindy had shut the door at the far end and flipped the dead bolt home with a sharp snick. She turned and smiled, slipping the gun into the back of her jeans as she walked over.

"We'll rig something up to secure that door leading to the stairwell. A guy would need a long ladder to climb back in that broken window. We'll check for that when we go outside." Cindy lifted the glass of wine and took a long sip.

Becky downed half the glass of wine, feeling it warm her throat despite the icy chill of the liquid. After that scare in the upstairs, she could use a drink to settle her nerves. "What about the doors leading to the other wings? We need to try them before we go to bed tonight. And if that lawyer's card turns up, I think we need to advise him that we're not alone in this place."

Melanie picked up her glass and clinked it against Cindy's and Becky's ending with the one still sitting alone on the counter. She smiled. "That's just it; if you'd ever listen to me. We're not alone. We've got Dara with us."

Chapter ELEVEN

BECKY SIGNALED WITH A SMALL SHAKE of her head for Cindy to let it go. Melanie had always been a bit odd about anything supernatural, and of course she was eating all of this up, reveling in being there. "To Dara. Our dear friend who left us much too soon."

Cindy and Melanie echoed her words, before downing the wine in their glasses. "To Dara." There were a few beats of silence, each picturing their friend, so full of life when they'd last seen her alive.

Cindy was the first to break the silence. "You know when she showed up in Chicago, so random like, crashing my dinner date with David, I was really pissed. I thought it was just one of her stunts, trying to get one up on me again. She could have had her pick of any guy in the room but she zeroed in on David."

Becky's voice was soft when she looked over at Cindy. "It sounds to me like she did you a favor."

"Absolutely. I know that now. But at the time it was hard. I was furious with her. She tried calling and texting me a few times but I ignored her." Cindy looked down into her empty glass. "Now I wish I'd talked to her before...well, you know."

Melanie put her hand on Cindy's, giving it a little squeeze. "She's probably happy hearing you say that."

This time not even a warning look from Becky could stop the explosive burst from Cindy. "Look! Will you stop with this ghostly shit? We're in the middle of nowhere with some guy trying to spook us, and that lawyer is probably itching for us to break that clause in Dara's will."

Becky could see that Melanie was on the verge of crying and Cindy's harshness wasn't helping. "Calm down, Cindy. We'll have another glass of wine and then finish securing this place. For now, we're together and safe in this kitchen. Besides which, you have the gun."

41

When she turned to Melanie it looked like she was lost in her own thoughts. She nudged her gently before she spoke. "When was the last time you were with Dara? I mean did she ever visit? I know you two were probably the closest of the four of us."

Melanie's face brightened, a smile breaking through. "She came out to Madison a few months before she passed on. We spent the day eating too much and walking along the beach. It was very last minute, and I had to call in sick at work to wrangle it. But there was no way I was gonna miss spending the day with her. She was still pretty sad about losing her dad. She spent the night." She cast a quick glance at Cindy but then forged ahead, her chin raised slightly. "We actually tried contacting his spirit that night."

Becky jumped in before Cindy lost it again. "The last time I saw Dara was at our reunion at the Sands in Vegas. Remember how she lost almost a hundred thousand dollars at the blackjack table? She never batted an eye over that."

Cindy snorted. "Neither did we when all room charges were comp'ed. I don't know about you but I work too damn hard for my money to piss it away like that. But she was a trust-fund kid. There was plenty more when that came from."

Melanie's eyes narrowed, and her words were clipped. "She was always generous with her money though. Remember at the end of the school year when cash was tight? She always picked up our share of the rent and made sure there was food and lots of booze. If not for her we'd have been living on Kraft Dinner."

Cindy nodded. "Yeah, I'll give her that. She was generous. Even in death, leaving her estate to us."

Becky eyed Cindy. Again, with the inheritance.

Setting her glass down, she nodded at Cindy. "We'd better see about securing any other ways of getting in here—those two other wings and that stairway. It's just after seven now." She turned to Melanie. "You'll be all right here starting dinner, won't you?"

"Of course. Go do what you need to do. I'm perfectly happy cooking. We can eat in the reception room." Melanie smiled and waved them away with a flutter of her fingers.

When they passed through the door and were out of Melanie's earshot, Cindy turned to Becky, lowering her voice as she spoke. "Is it just me, or does Melanie seem more assertive now? She actually snapped at me a few times since we've been here."

Becky nodded slowly. "Yeah, I noticed that as well." She risked a quip to lighten the mood, "Maybe she's channeling Dara. That's one thing you could always count on with Dara. She'd be right in your face if she disagreed with something you'd said or done."

"No kidding." Cindy's eyes narrowed. "But that visit with Melanie...trying to contact her dead *father*? And then there's the letter to us. It's like she knew she was going to die." Cindy straightened, pulling back while peering at Becky. "Maybe she and Melanie were more alike than we'd ever noticed."

"Well, they roomed together the first year, in residence. I could never understand why Dara was so fond of Mel. They were polar opposites. Dara outgoing, the party animal, while Mel—"

"Mel the Mouse."

A series of piercing screeches sounded from outside the front door. Becky's eyes flashed wide looking over at Cindy. When the noise continued, she could make out a rustling sound and a distinct "'caw'." She rushed to the door and opened it in time to see three large crows take flight, leaving the source of the squabble in a bloody heap on the stone step. The tiny leg of a field mouse jerked once before it became perfectly still.

"Eeew. gross." Cindy turned away in disgust.

The poor thing. Becky sprinted out, ready to put the thing out of its misery if it moved again. But its black eyes were glazed and its mouth open revealing a pink tongue. Pieces of the skin on its side had been ripped or plucked off, revealing a gaping red hole. She bent to pick it up, using the sleeve of her sweatshirt to grip its tail. She tossed it over beside the balcony that was off to the side, overlooking the lake and gardens.

"There." She looked up at the sky for any sign of the crows but only a few clouds scuttled, almost indistinguishable from the gray gloom. It looked like a storm was brewing which would probably roll in later on.

She joined Cindy who still stood in the doorway. "Let's get this place secured. I need more wine, and fast, if I'm going to sleep tonight." Without saying another word, Cindy strode across the reception area to the door that led to a side wing. She tried the handle, and Becky cringed seeing it swing open so easily.

It had been too much to hope for that it would be locked with a dead bolt on the reception side.

Becky headed to the other side of the room where a door led to the third wing of the building. Again, when she tried it, it opened after a few yanks. She peered over at Cindy. "The only way we're going to be able to secure these doors is to nail them shut. I don't suppose you also brought a toolkit in that oversized trunk."

"I've got a sewing kit and complete manicure set but no hammer or nails." Cindy's eyes squinted as she stood looking at the door. "But maybe the crew that was here left some nails. We need to check outside. There might be something of use in that garage or the other outbuilding."

Becky groaned at the thought of going out there. That intruder was still around, maybe hiding there waiting to ambush them or something. But Cindy was already on her way across the room, plucking the gun from the back of her pants.

"C'mon! Let's see what we can find while we have daylight." Cindy pulled the front door open and stepped outside.

When Becky followed, she peered up at the sky before scampering down the wide steps. Dark thunderclouds had moved in fast. It looked like it could start raining any minute. Her heartbeat quickened as she raced to catch up to Cindy.

When they rounded the end of the main part of the resort, she could see the garage. This was definitely going to be a shot in the dark, seeing the dilapidated building with the roof looking like it would cave in at any time. The contractors hadn't gotten around to fixing anything there, so it wasn't likely they'd find any building supplies.

Cindy ducked under the edge of the twisted metal of the garage door and stood holding the gun before her. She called over her shoulder to Becky, "I'll keep an eye out here while you rummage around to see if you can find any screws or nails."

The thought of going inside the dim area, past that rusted hunk of junk tractor held little appeal. Becky grumbled a reply, "Even if I'm lucky enough to find a nail, we still don't have a hammer or tools." She scowled at Cindy as she passed by her.

"Let me worry about that. You didn't grow up with older brothers. It wouldn't be the first time I hammered a nail with just a rock."

Becky rolled her eyes and stepped forward slowly. There was a workbench strewn with busted boards and the metal parts of some motor, all connected by gossamer sheets of spider webs. Her nostrils flared as her hands swept the cobwebs clear. After shaking the sticky threads off her fingers, she leaned in peering down at layers of dust and grease on the old wooden surface. She moved a few old, crumbling boxes aside, but there were only mice droppings and dirt to be seen.

"Try that drawer to your left. There might be something there we can use."

Becky looked down and saw the drawer. When she grabbed the handle, the screw holding the one side of it gave way. She hooked her fingers in the small crevice between the bench and the drawer and gave it a sharp yank. The rattle of metal clicking against metal followed. There in the side of the drawer was a box of four-inch nails bound in a lump of rust. She tapped the bundle and scooped up a handful in the center which weren't completely coated in orange flakes.

"Got some!" When she turned, Cindy was no longer standing in the opening of the doorway. Her breath hitched in her throat for a moment. "Cindy?"

Chapter TWELVE

BECKY RACED OUTSIDE. Where the hell had Cindy gone? That intruder...

"Over here!" Cindy stood looking up at the wing of the building closest to the garage. It was in rough shape with many broken windows showing through a mottled surface of amber stucco and cement.

Becky edged closer to her friend, her voice dropping to a whisper, "Did you see him?" She peered hard along each floor of windows trying to see any sign of movement. Dark holes, like missing teeth, were the only things that showed in the fading light of the day.

"I heard something and so I rushed out. But damned if there's any sign of anyone." Cindy glanced at her and then signaled with a jerk of her head. "We'd better get in there and check on Mel. You've got the nails?"

"Yeah. But what about a rock—"

"The kitchen probably has a meat tenderizer. We'll use that to pound in the nails." Cindy turned and led the way back around the building to the main entrance.

As she followed, Becky noticed the rental car parked near the end of the circular drive. She kind of wished she'd left it out front closer to the main set of stairs.

Looking at Cindy ahead of her she ventured a thought that had been niggling in the back of her mind. "It probably wouldn't hurt to place a call to 911 and see if they'd send a police car out to check the premises. Surely the lawyer couldn't object to that."

Cindy turned on her and sneered. "Do you really want to take that chance? Seriously, Becky. We'll secure all the entrances and we'll be fine. I've also got a gun. Mel's not worried about any intruder, and there's no way I'm going to jeopardize that ten mill. Just relax, okay?"

Becky could feel her cheeks get warmer being chastised by Cindy. Well, there was no way she'd stop her from calling home to talk to

Hank. At the very least she should let him know she had arrived safely. As for the ten million dollars...well they still didn't have that check in hand yet. It would sure make things easier if that money actually came through.

If she and Cindy were right and that lawyer was up to something there was more than one way to skin a cat.

"Okay. We'll tough it out so that we don't void the terms of the will. But!" She gripped Cindy's forearm and gave it a small shake. "We take turns tonight standing guard. You and me. Mel wouldn't be interested—"

Cindy's eyes had become slits and she jumped in. "We can't trust her. If she heard anything she'd assume it was Dara's ghost or some other shit. No, it's up to us, Becky. You take the first watch. Wake me at three and I'll cover the rest of it. It will be like the old days, sleep deprived, studying for finals."

"I don't think we should even tell Melanie what we're doing." It wasn't a pleasant thought but Becky had to put it out there. "Melanie might sabotage our efforts to secure the place, getting up and opening doors, maybe even wandering down to the lake to commune with Dara."

Cindy's eyes opened wider and she nodded slowly. "You're right. She's so determined that Dara is here. Her behavior could pose a danger with some thug trying to terrorize, if not maybe *kill* us." She smiled at Becky. "We always were a good team, you and I, Becks. We worked hard for everything we got, right from the get-go."

"Working-class heroes. That's us." Becky smiled, remembering how they'd spent their first year in university, rooming together. Neither of them got through school without working two jobs in the summer break. Cindy's dad was a bricklayer while her own father had barely scraped by selling used cars.

When they entered the reception area, locking the door behind her, Becky saw that Melanie was just coming out the kitchen door. She carried a bottle of wine in one hand while her other held the single red rose in a vase.

Cindy called out to her. "Hey Mel, did you happen to notice a mallet or meat tenderizer in the kitchen?" She paused, slipping the gun back into the back waistband of her jeans. "We found nails to secure those other doors tight."

Melanie's smile was wistful when she set the vase on the table. "You'll find the meat tenderizer in the sink. I used it on the chicken so you might want to give it a rinse. But..." This time there was no mistaking the look in her eyes. She grinned. "It won't matter, you know. Why not accept the fact that the four of us are together again and try to cherish this weekend? She wanted us to celebrate her life and give her a good send-off? That's what she wrote in the letter."

Cindy nodded, but when she was out of Melanie's line of sight, she made a face that only Becky could see, her forefinger making a circle sweep next to her temple. She then disappeared into the kitchen.

Becky quickly turned to Melanie. "That letter she wrote... Cindy and I were talking about it. You think she knew she was going to die here, Mel? What did you make of that?"

Melanie folded her arms over her chest, looking down at the rose. A petal dropped onto the gleaming wood surface, highlighted by the chandelier overhead that now lit the room. "She had that dream, yet she came here anyway. I think she was torn. The rational Dara, the one following this quest to breathe life back into this place won out over her instincts. I wish she'd called me. I would have urged her to let this place go."

Becky rubbed her hands along her upper arms feeling the chill in the air now that night had descended. It was early autumn, yet the nights held a hint of the winter nipping at its heels. A low rumbling of thunder sounded. She looked out the window at the horizon; the storm was still a way off in the mountains.

Becky sighed. "Well, she didn't. Instead, Dara drowned here. Whatever possessed her to stay here alone, never mind swimming in the lake by herself? She may have found the place charming, but to me it's just a rundown hotel, better torn down than revamped."

Melanie brightened. "Maybe I'll buy it for back taxes once the government owns it. I'd have enough money to continue the work. I'll have a better idea about that after this weekend. I feel Dara's presence here, even if you and Cindy don't."

Becky shook her head. Even ignoring the spiritualism aspect of Melanie's plan, it was a ridiculous idea. "But Mel, this is entirely out of character for you. You're a librarian, not an entrepreneur. You'd waste that money and be miserable doing it."

Mel persisted. "You're forgetting her premonition in the letter. She was worried she'd become trapped in some afterlife state. She wanted us to free her if that happened."

"What the hell are you talking about?"

Mel's face went icy. "You didn't hear what the lawyer said when he was reading the letter; you got too hung up on the money." She shook her head sadly. "Dara said we have to give her a good send-off or she's going to be trapped here!"

Becky felt her face flush. Yeah, there was something like that in the letter. Too damn bad the lawyer didn't leave it with them.

Before they could say anything else, Cindy popped out from the kitchen carrying the meat tenderizer. She looked from Melanie to Becky as she wandered over to take the nails from her. "What are you two scheming? You might want to check on that meat in the oven, Melanie. And bring some glasses out when you return."

Melanie gave her head a quick shake, signaling with her eyes to Becky to keep their earlier conversation private. Cindy would be more vocal in giving Mel an earful about her harebrained idea about Dara's soul getting trapped. She'd find a time to talk to Melanie over the weekend and convince her how crazy the notion of buying the resort was. And she wasn't giving any credence to Dara's spirit or essence or whatever being trapped there. That was total nonsense.

Becky's hand went to her forehead, giving it a light tap. "Shit! I have to call Hank, and let him know we arrived safe and sound."

Cindy chortled before turning to the task at hand, toe-nailing a spike through the first door. "I'm sure he'll be thrilled when you tell him about the money!" She began hammering the nail with sharp taps.

Melanie had gone back into the kitchen, and Becky turned to go to the wing where her bedroom was. When she stepped through the door, she glanced in the wastebasket on her way by to grab her bag from the dresser. The jasmine wasn't there. Her gaze darted to the bed where the sprig once more graced the center of the pillow.

She let out a deep sigh. Of course, this time it had been Melanie restoring what she thought were "'Dara's touches.'" If she checked on Cindy's room, it would be a sure bet that her yellow rose would once more be on the pillow there.

She plucked the phone from her purse and clicked the speed dial connecting to her husband's phone.

Chapter THIRTEEN

BECKY RUBBED HER TEMPLE as she wandered back to the reception area. Cindy was just finishing pounding in the nails on the second door when she entered the room.

She turned and grinned at Becky. "All set! There's no way of getting these doors open without breaking them down, and, for sure we'd hear that." She set the mallet on the large table and poured a couple glasses of wine. "What'd Hank say about the money? I bet he was totally floored by that!"

Becky flopped into the chair she'd sat in previously that day. "There was no answer when I called him." She forced a smile seeing the puzzlement in Cindy's eyes. "He probably went out to the store and forgot to take his phone with him. That's Hank, the epitome of an absent-minded professor."

Cindy rolled her eyes and smirked. "Nice to see he's so concerned for your safety. The jerk." She took a long swallow of wine, still eyeing Becky over the rim of the glass. "Things are good between you, aren't they? I mean he's not screwing around on you, is he?"

Becky almost spewed out the wine she'd just sipped, quickly covering her lips with the back of her other hand. She smiled. "Hank? God no! My biggest competition for his attention is research! He's just published a paper on the role of institutions creating political bias."

Cindy held up her hand, "Okay, okay. Just don't try to explain what the hell that study's about." She grinned. "Well, maybe later. I'm sure it will put me right to sleep."

Becky didn't notice Melanie enter the room until she sat down at the head of the table.

The young blond woman leaned over the table peering at Becky and Cindy. "Surely, you're not planning on going to bed before midnight. I think we should be awake for Dara's birthday..."—she glanced at the watch on her wrist—"...in four hours and ten minutes, to be exact."

Becky shrugged. It wouldn't be a problem for her since she'd agreed to take first watch tonight. Which meant she probably should ease up on having any more wine after this glass.

Cindy shook her head, glancing over at Melanie. "I'm probably going to be in bed, asleep shortly after we eat. We'll still be here tomorrow, Mel, on Dara's birthday like she asked. There's no rule that says we have to be awake when that day arrives."

Melanie's chin rose, and she looked off to the side before speaking. "True. But considering that we were her best friends, it's not such a great sacrifice. I mean, she never even lived to celebrate it."

"Look, Mel, we all miss her." Cindy glanced at Becky. "The place is totally secure now and we have to keep it that way. No one leaves the building till morning, okay? We stay inside where it's safe."

Becky reached over and placed her hand on Melanie's, ignoring Cindy. She could see that this was really important to Mel, being awake when midnight rolled over. "I'll stay up with you, Mel. I'm really kind of a night owl anyway. Remember?"

Becky sniffed. "Thanks, Becky. I knew I could count on you to understand. We were always closer to Dara than Cindy ever was." She flashed a look at Cindy and rose to her feet. "I'd better check on the rice. Everything else is done. I'll bring dinner in."

Becky watched the ramrod stiff set of Melanie's back as she strode from the room. She looked over at Cindy. "I'll be awake anyway. At least this way I can keep an eye on her." It might also be a better opportunity to talk Mel out of that harebrained scheme of buying this dump.

But Cindy's attention was focused on the bottle of wine, her fingers plucking at the edge of the label. "I don't think that's true, Becky. Dara and I had our differences, but I was close to her too. Every bit as close as you were to her." She glanced at Becky and her voice became even lower. "You and I knew that Melanie always had kind of a crush on Dara. Shit, even Dara knew it. And with Mel's mom coming out of the closet..."

Cindy was hitting on what Becky had always suspected. Melanie was in denial about it, but everything pointed to the fact that she was more into girls than guys. She'd never shown the slightest interest in dating guys.

Becky thought back to that first year in college. "Can you imagine how hard that was on Melanie? She was away from home, first year university and Mom moves in with her secret lesbian lover."

"Not to mention, selling the house and moving to a big city." Cindy shook her head, deliberately peeling the labels away in long strips. "Presto. Every root that grounded Melanie evaporated overnight. It was almost like her mother couldn't wait for Mel to leave so she could begin her *own* life."

Becky let out a long sigh. "Dara got her through that year. There's no doubt about that. I know the sacrifices Dara made, limiting her own social life to be there for Mel." She leaned in closer to Cindy, casting a quick glance at the door before continuing. "She tried to kill herself. Dara told me about it. If Dara hadn't skipped a class and gone home early that day, Melanie might not be around. But don't let on you know that."

Cindy's eyes were round, watching Becky. "I won't. But that certainly explains her obsessive behavior. Dara literally saved her life. Dara's death was sad for you and me, but it probably broke Melanie's heart."

Becky nodded. "Which is also why she can't let go, with all her talk of Dara being here."

At the crackle and sizzle above her, Becky's gaze shot to the chandelier. The lights pulsed and flickered for a few beats. The hissing stopped and the lights became steady, casting shadows in the far recesses of the room. She let out a long, slow breath, only now aware that she'd been holding it.

A loud crack of thunder followed, shaking the floor under her feet and she flinched.

"Shit! That scared the hell out of me!" Cindy picked up the wine bottle to top up her glass. "The storm must be right overhead now. We probably should look for candles or something in case the power goes out."

Melanie pushed the kitchen door open and entered, carrying a large silver tray before her. Steam wafted above a bowl of rice and plate of chicken breasts. Beside that platter was a clear glass salad bowl, already tossed. The smell of lemon and curry filled Becky's nostrils. She rose to her feet. "Can I give you a hand, Mel?"

"No, I got this." She set the tray down and began unloading the dishes of food, ending with plates and cutlery, setting each before the two women.

Becky noticed the two plates still there. Melanie set one at the empty place across from her, replete with fork, knife and a cloth napkin.

Her gut sank, realizing that Melanie was setting a place for Dara.

Chapter FOURTEEN

CINDY STARED AT THE VACANT PLACE SETTING for a few beats before exploding. "*Come on!*" Her head fell back, and she looked up at the ceiling.

"I knew you'd have something to say about that." Melanie took her seat and smiled at Cindy. "Tough shit. Just think of it as a reminder. This weekend is about her, not you. Not me. And not Becky."

Becky rose to her feet. Although she agreed with Cindy's sentiment that Mel was crossing a line into moribund, the bickering was getting on her nerves. "Mel? Did you see any candles anywhere in the kitchen? With this storm and all, we might—"

"I brought candles." Melanie seemed to brighten at the question. She got up and called over her shoulder as she walked across the room to their wing's entrance. "Help yourselves but leave me some food, Cindy!"

Cindy watched the door bang shut behind Melanie before she spoke. "Does that include Dara's portion? You think Mel's going to pile food onto that extra plate for her?"

Becky gave her head a small shake, taking her seat. But a glance at the chicken on the platter showed only three pieces. Apparently, Melanie wasn't that far gone.

"Just dish it up, will you?" She shot a direct look at Cindy. "Try to be patient, would you? We've got another night here, and I'd just as soon not have it erode into a catfight."

Once more the lights flickered. This time darkness shrouded them. The clap of thunder was immediate, making Becky jump. Oh shit. She'd left her cell phone in the room. She could have used its light.

A bright beam flashed in her eyes almost blinding her. Cindy held her phone high, shining it down on the table and then across the room where Melanie had gone.

"I'll go and see that she's all right. She's probably stumbling into walls. She's liable to break her neck or something." Cindy got to her feet and then strode across the room, leaving Becky in total darkness.

For a few minutes Becky sat in the dark, thrumming her fingers on the arms of her chair. The rain had started too, pelting against the windows in a steady torrent. What was keeping those two? Maybe Cindy was retrieving the other cell phone for backup. That had to be it. But still, sitting there in the dark by herself, waiting while the storm thundered on made her skin prickle.

A flash of lightning lit the room. In that fraction of a second, a woman's shape was illuminated in the chair across from her. Becky froze, her heart leaping in her chest. The booming crack of thunder barely registered in her ears as she sat there hardly daring to breathe.

That woman was sitting at Dara's place setting. Oh God.

Her fingers gripped the arms of the chair as she sat there unable to move a muscle. Melanie thought Dara was here. Was she right? Had that flash illuminated her spirit? Oh shit.

No. No. No. You're a scientist, Rebecca. Dr. Rebecca Sloan. You know better than this. It could very well have been some afterimage stored in her retinas. The last person she looked at was Cindy before everything went dark. And Cindy and Dara had similar features, shoulder-length hair, the same high forehead and sculpted cheekbones. It had to be some trick of her eyes.

Dara was dead.

Even so, she wished her friends would hurry the hell up with those candles and cell phones.

"Cindy? Mel?" Her voice cracked when she called out to them. She listened hard but there was only the patter of the rain hitting the windows.

This was all Melanie's fault, with all that talk of Dara being there. It was no wonder she was nervous, especially when the storm knocked the power out. She was reverting to primal fear, and she was much too educated and rational to sink to that level. It had been an afterimage imprinted on her retinas. That's all.

At the sound of footsteps to her left and a shaft of light coming through the doorway, her grip on the arms of the chair relaxed.

"Got your phone for you, Becks. Although we should conserve use of it. Who knows how long the power will be out." Cindy shone her flashlight app on the table while Melanie set Becky's phone next to her.

Melanie's eyes glittered in the spark of light from the match she held to the wick of the candle. "I love beeswax candles. You can smell a hint of honey as they burn." She set the thick, yellow candle in the center of the table and took a seat.

Becky couldn't help peering at the spot where she thought she'd seen the woman. Of course, there was nothing there except the white plate and the silverware next to it, the low light sparkling on the empty wineglass. This was silly. It was a given that there'd be nothing there.

She took a deep breath, leaning over the table. "Dinner smells delicious. I'm not sure about smelling honey, but I definitely smell lemon and chicken." When another petal of the rose fluttered down onto the table, she edged back a little in her chair. Why had Melanie put that damn rose there?

Cindy took a bite of the chicken, easing forward. "Mmmm. I didn't realize how hungry I was until now. Good job, Mel." She poured another glass of wine and then offered some to Becky and Melanie.

Becky put her hand over the top of the glass. "No. I'm good. I'll just finish what's here and call it quits." She still had first watch, and the wine wouldn't help her to stay awake, even though her nerves could use it. That had been a silly fright, thinking she'd seen Dara's ghost.

Ghost. Yeah, right.

"Just half a glass for me." Melanie held her glass out, reaching across the table. "Do you remember the time that Dara was dating those identical twins? Remember that football game the one took her to, where they got smashed?"

Cindy snorted almost choking on the wine. "Oh my God. She got up to go to the bathroom and forgot where they were seated. She ended up sitting in another section with the second twin who was stone-cold sober. She couldn't figure out how he sobered up so fast. When they ended up back at their place, the other brother was there, totally pissed that she'd deserted him."

Becky shook her head. "As I recall, there was a huge fistfight between the guys, and she dumped both of them on the spot." She laughed, cutting another wedge of chicken. "Family reunions must be tense for that pair."

Cindy sighed. "Yeah, that was one she lorded over me. I never dated twins let alone having them fistfight over me. And they weren't hard on the eyes either. Whatever happened to them? There might still be time for me to match Dara's scorecard."

The memory brought a smile to Becky's lips. "You two! If it wasn't always competing for the best grades, it was comparing the number of notches on the bedpost." She looked over at Melanie. "How did we manage to graduate, let alone stay sane with those two around? How many times did we wander into the kitchen in the morning to be met by some hung-over jock rummaging around in our fridge?"

"More than a few times..."

"Damn right!" Becky made a face at Cindy. "After a while I never even tried to remember their names."

Cindy tapped Becky's arm. "Not true! You remembered Alex's name! Remember Alex? Six four, all muscle with those droopy bedroom eyes that made every girl drool? Oh yeah. You remember him all right! And you'll also remember that I dated him first!"

Melanie's voice was soft and far away. "That was until Dara got home from Europe. It was Christmas break. Remember? She and her dad went to the Alps to ski that year. I can still see her coming in the door, her skin slightly tanned from the winter sun and air, her dark hair streaming over that white ski jacket."

"Yes. Dara was beautiful." Unlike Cindy, Becky had never felt threatened or intimidated by that fact. Becky's own beauty was more the girl-next-door variety, not glamorous but definitely there nonetheless. It explained why out of the four of them, she was the only one who had married. Cindy held such an elevated opinion of herself it would be hard for any guy to measure up. And Mel...well, she was who she was.

"She told me once that she'd never be good enough." Melanie had finished her meal and pushed it away slightly. "Her father had always wanted a son. You know those eastern Europeans needing heirs. She tried her best to please him. But when her mother died in that car accident he shut himself off from her emotionally."

Cindy rose to her feet, scooping up the empty plates. "Yes. It was a shame how he treated her." She glanced at Becky. "Can you light the way for me to take these into the kitchen. We'll do the cleanup in the morning when we have light."

Becky grabbed her cell phone and shone the light walking next to Cindy. "Thanks for making dinner, Mel. It was really good."

Of course, it was Becky who probably knew the most about Dara's relationship with her family. They all had confided in Becky, which is most likely the reason she ended up with a major in psychotherapy. It made sense that Dara had also confided in Mel. Strange that someone as self-absorbed as Cindy had picked up on it though.

When they returned from the kitchen Melanie held the rose close to her nose, her head dipped. Becky squeezed Mel's shoulder on the way by, trying to comfort her.

"*What the hell?*"

Becky looked over at Cindy. She held the empty wineglass, the one at Dara's place setting, before the flame of the candle. There was a smattering of wine in the bottom of the glass but it was the rim that shot an arrow of fear through Becky's chest.

A smudge of lipstick cupped the area just below the top edge. Even in the low light of the candle she could see that it was a scarlet red—the exact shade Dara had always worn.

They both looked at Melanie. But Melanie's face was devoid of any makeup except for a dash of mascara. Her lips were a pale shade, hard to distinguish from the alabaster tone of her cheeks. Definitely no trace of red lipstick.

"I know you did this, Mel!" Cindy set the glass down in front of Melanie. "You've got that tube of lipstick in your pocket. You put that lipstick on the glass and then cleaned your lips before we got back."

Melanie's eyes narrowed and her head jerked back. "You're crazy! Why would I do something like that?" She picked the glass up and examined it closely, peering at the print of lips highlighted in red. "That's definitely Dara's shade. Chanel Rouge Allure, if I recall. Remember her vamping around the house in a flimsy nightgown, singing that old song by Marlena Deitrich. "Lily Marlene"—that was it."

Becky felt like her eyes were about to pop out onto her cheekbones, staring at the glass. Yes. It was the exact shade that Dara wore. But why would Melanie put it there?

She could picture the scene Melanie had mentioned. Dara had even sung the song in its original German version, totally hamming it up, slinking along the sofa like a cat. They'd just finished the last exam and had been celebrating with copious amounts of gin that night.

"Underneath the lantern, by the barrack gate, Darling I remember—"

"Stop singing that!" Cindy turned on Melanie like a viper. "You're trying to scare us, convince us that Dara is here! It won't work, Mel. So just cut it out!"

A flash of lightning lit the room once more, and immediately Becky's gaze shot to the empty place setting. This time the clap of thunder was like a gunshot.

Cindy flopped down in the chair she'd vacated and finished the wine in her glass. "Shit, I wish the power would come back on—especially with her acting so damn creepy." She glared at Melanie, who just returned her gaze with a small smile.

With the tension in the air, there was no way Becky was going to mention what she thought she'd seen earlier. Mel would eat it up, but Cindy was bound to hit the roof. It had been an afterimage, that's all. Besides, Cindy was probably right about the lipstick. If they searched Mel, they'd find it.

When Melanie once more began humming that nostalgic tune, Becky barked at her, "That's enough, Melanie." The look in Mel's eyes was defiant but she stopped humming.

Chapter FIFTEEN

CINDY GLANCED AT HER PHONE, "Shit. It's only a little after nine. This is way too early for me to go to bed and that's the last of this wine."

Melanie stood up, signaling with a snap of her fingers for Becky to hand her the cell phone. "There're at least six bottles in the fridge. I wouldn't mind having a bit more either." She fished in the pocket of her jeans, and when her hand emerged, she held a flat tin can. "I grew this myself. All organic if you'd like to smoke a few joints."

Becky held her hand up like a traffic cop. "Not for me. But if you see a bottle of water or soda in the fridge, I'll take that." It had been years since she'd done weed, and she intended to keep it that way. Hell on the short-term memory with a dash of paranoia thrown in, was how she remembered it. There was enough paranoia going down right now with the strange happenings and Melanie's behavior.

"I'll join you in some weed, Mel. That will definitely put me right to sleep." Cindy watched Melanie go into the kitchen before she turned to Becky.

She leaned in closer and her voice lowered. "I'm glad you're staying up to babysit her. That stunt with the lipstick...well, it just proves how unstable she is, trying to convince us that Dara's here. She even knew the name of it, just like that. "She snapped her fingers before her face.

Becky shook her head slowly. "That doesn't mean anything. I remembered it too." Of course, Cindy wouldn't know the name. If it didn't concern Cindy directly, it didn't exist.

"Whatever." She picked up the wineglass, examining it in the low light of the candle. Her thumb rubbed the lipstick mark but the imprint remained. There wasn't even a trace of red on her thumb. "What the hell? It's like it's etched in the glass. How'd she manage that?"

For a moment Becky could only watch the glass silently, recalling the woman outlined in the flash of lightning earlier. If Melanie had put it there, that lipstick should have smudged or marked Cindy's thumb. Her eyes opened wider in horror. What if...

No. No. No. The place was getting to her, and the storm outside wasn't helping. There was a plausible explanation for the impervious lipstick. She sat taller, confident that in the cold, hard light of day she'd find out how Melanie had done it.

She looked up when the kitchen door opened, and Melanie appeared, carrying a fresh bottle of wine and a bottle of water.

"No pop, but a whole case of bottled water." She handed Becky the water and then leaned over to refill Cindy's glass. But she didn't stop there. She also poured more wine into Dara's glass before filling her own.

Becky gave Cindy's leg a small nudge with her foot under the table, noticing that she was about to comment on Melanie's actions. If Melanie felt the need to continue her charade, then what did it really matter? They'd get through this weekend and laugh about that later. Maybe even Mel would too.

Melanie took a joint out, lit it and took a long drag from it before holding it out to Cindy. The pungent, almost skunky aroma drifted into Becky's nostrils as the doobie went by her. She sat back a little and turned her head.

"You grow this stuff, Mel? Aren't you worried about getting caught? Recreational use is still not legal in Connecticut. Or has that changed? It's hard to keep up with all the laws around it." Becky uncapped her water and took a long swig.

Melanie shrugged before a long stream of smoke from her nostrils caused the candle light to flicker. "I grow it in my apartment with lights. It's just for my use, and I don't smoke in public. My cat's certainly not going to turn me in." She smiled. "He chewed some buds one time and his eyes were crossed for two days."

Cindy chuckled, letting out a burst of smoke. "Poor Mr. Whiskas. Did he get the munchies?" She took another drag before handing the joint back to Mel.

Melanie giggled. "No. But he slept an awful lot. I keep my plants up on a very high shelf now."

Becky gazed at Melanie, watching her loosen up and smile. "So, do you have many friends there, Mel? Seeing anyone at all?"

Melanie nodded. "Yeah. I go out once in a while. There're a group of friends with similar interests." The look on her face became wistful, looking down into the glass of wine.

"So, any love interest?" Cindy leaned closer. "I think that's what Becky was trying to get around to. Are you getting laid?" Cindy glanced at Becky and gave her leg a nudge with her foot.

But Becky didn't want to put Melanie on the spot. If Melanie wanted them to know more about her private life, she'd open up on her own. She threw a look at Cindy. "It's always sex with you. Why don't you tell us about *your* latest conquests? Melanie's got friends she goes out with. That's all I wanted to know, not torrid details."

But Melanie spoke before Cindy had a chance to counter. "There's one guy I see. He's a fireman, built like a brick shithouse. We get together about once a month."

Cindy and Becky exchanged another look. A guy? Becky leaned closer. "Just once a month? Is he married or something?"

Melanie shook her head. "No. Not that I know... No ring or *anything*. It works for us." She smiled again, a sly smile hinting that the subject was personal and none of their business.

Cindy took another hit of the joint, bringing it down to a small roach. She looked at the burning end, then with a flick of her hand, tossed it into Dara's wineglass. Even in the dim light of the flickering candle, Becky could see that her eyes were slightly glazed. Cindy was feeling the effects of the wine and that joint.

Making a small cough, Cindy said, "We always thought that...well...that you were *gay,* Mel. Yet, you're seeing some hunky fireman?" She picked up her glass of wine and drained it.

For a few moments, Becky sat still as a statue. Cindy had just blurted that out without a thought to poor Melanie's feelings!

"*Gay?*" Melanie's voice boomed through the air. "Not that there's anything wrong with that. Some of my friends have come out, but let me assure you, I'm not even remotely interested in women sexually. But I sure as hell was never interested in the Neanderthals that you and Dara dated. I was at school to get a degree, not a husband!"

Melanie turned to Becky and her head dipped a bit. "No offense, Becky. I know that's where you met Hank."

"It's okay." Becky murmured. There were times lately when she'd questioned the wisdom of that decision. Maybe she'd married too young. Cindy was still playing the field, free to do what she wanted, go wherever she pleased. Even Mel had some hot fireman on the string.

Cindy's hands flew up in front of her chest. "Sorry! We were wrong." She lurched a little to the side when she rose to her feet. "I'm going to bed. I'm starting to see double Melanies sitting at the table."

"It's pretty potent grass, Cindy. I should have warned you."

"No shit, Sherlock."

Becky jumped from her seat, seeing Cindy about to stagger to the side. She grabbed her friend's arm to steady her. "I'll walk you to your room." She held the cell phone high, lighting the way across the room. "I'll be right back, Mel."

As she passed through the door, keeping a swaying Cindy upright, Mel's voice drifted into her ear. "Take your time. We're not going anywhere."

They were almost at Cindy's room when Becky broached the subject. "Maybe you should give me the gun, Cindy. I'll give it back to you when I wake you at three."

Cindy burst out laughing, her hand fumbling for the doorknob. "No way! You don't know anything about guns, Becks. You'd probably end up shooting yourself or Mel if I give it to you. No, the Glock stays with me."

"Well, put it on the night table beside you at least. You can't sleep with that thing sticking down your pants." She watched Cindy's eyes blinking slowly. It wouldn't be that long before her friend passed out. She could always sneak back in to get it. If Cindy didn't like that, too bad. A fat lot of good it'd be sitting on the table if someone tried to break in.

"Sure." Cindy yanked the weapon from her jeans and set it down slowly. The next second she fell forward, landing on her stomach on the bed. Her head rose and it looked like she might try to get up but then she flopped back like a dead fish.

Becky picked up the gun and tucked it into her waistband the same way she'd seen her friend do it. It still felt warm from Cindy's body. And, like a hot water bottle on a cold night, it felt soothing. She smirked to herself recalling the Beatles' tune "'Happiness Is A Warm Gun.'"

Back in the hallway, she jumped when one of the bedroom doors was flung open. She jerked the flashlight out before her as her other hand dropped to the gun in her waistband.

When Melanie stepped out from her room, Becky let out a whoosh of air. "Shit Mel! What the hell are you doing?" Her heart was going like a racehorse, and her hand shook pulling it away from the gun.

"I thought I'd put my PJs on. That's all." Melanie tilted her head and raised an eyebrow. "God, you're jumpy as a cat. Sure you don't want any of my weed?" Glancing over Becky's shoulder she asked, "Did you get Cindy settled?"

They headed back to the dining room, and Becky fell into stride beside her friend. "She's out cold. Didn't even bother to get undressed."

She placed her hand on Melanie's arm. "I hope you weren't upset about Cindy's comment, that we thought you were gay."

Melanie snorted. "Hardly. Dara made that mistake as well...thinking I was gay." She was silent for a few moments examining Becky's face. "You didn't know. I thought out of all of us she would have confided in you."

"Know what, Mel?"

"*Dara* was gay...or at least bisexual. She came on to me one night during first year. She was drunk and apologized the next day for her actions, but the funny thing was...it never changed our relationship. She was still kind and sweet to me even though I'd rejected her. I loved her as a sister, nothing more." She pushed the door open and held it for Becky, shining her light in the doorway.

"Cindy never knew that either." Becky felt disoriented walking across the large room to the table. In all the years she'd known Dara this was something that she'd never picked up on. Like Cindy, she'd had her suspicions about Melanie but never Dara.

"No, Cindy doesn't know. And if it's all the same to you, let's keep it between ourselves, okay?" Melanie took her seat at the table. She looked over at the place setting that she'd set for Dara. "She doesn't mind me telling you this."

Despite her better judgment to not encourage Melanie in her macabre fantasy, curiosity won out—especially after the lipstick and her fleeting image in the flash of lightning. "You really are convinced she's here. What I don't get is why *we're* here. Why would she put us through this to receive an inheritance?"

Melanie turned to Becky. "She needs us, Beck. She knew that we're the only ones who loved her for who she was. Loved her not for her money or what she could do for us but just for the wonderful person she is, or was. That love will set her free from this place."

"But why did she think she'd be stuck here? Hell, how did she even know she would die here unless she had some kind of death wish? Did she, Mel?" She stared at Melanie, trying to read her face in the low light of the candle. From the latest bombshell she'd revealed, Melanie knew Dara better than any of them.

"No. Dara didn't commit suicide. I'd stake my life on that. It's this place that killed her. Don't you feel it?" She gestured at the area. "There's a heaviness in the air here. When you and Cindy were playing detective searching the upstairs, I was getting dinner ready. All the time I was in the kitchen I felt like someone was watching me. A couple of times I turned suddenly and I swear there was a shadow. But it vanished quickly."

The place is creepy; I'll grant you that. But haunted? That's pretty far-fetched." Becky still wasn't willing to give credibility to the image she'd also seen. All this talk of shadows at the edge of your vision, pointed to an overactive imagination more than anything else.

Melanie's eyes were hard gazing at Becky. "What about the letter she wrote? She must have felt the same things that I've experienced since coming here. There's something in this resort that doesn't want us here. Somehow it managed to kill Dara."

"She drowned, Mel. She may have had some kind of premonition of her death but it was a case of being stupid and going swimming by herself." Becky glanced over at the spot where Dara's place setting lay. The glass now held beads of condensation from the chilled wine as well as that imprint of lips. Seeing it sit there untouched by anyone but Mel was a testament to the pathetic loss of Dara's life. Becky sighed. "Or maybe it was worse."

"What's that supposed to mean?" Mel's voice was high pitched.

Becky shrugged, looking away. What the hell. "Maybe...maybe she wanted to die?"

She turned back to Melanie, determined to put an end to all this ghostly talk.

At the small thud and the sound of glass shattering, Becky's head jerked back to that empty place setting. A puddle of wine spread over the dark wood while shards of glass were all that remained of the crystal goblet. Her heart leapt into her throat while the small hairs on her arms tingled. The chair was empty and neither she nor Mel had made a move to have caused that glass to tip.

"See?" Mel was smiling once more, totally at ease with the situation. Her eyes glinted in the light of the candle.

"How? You must have jostled the table...or..." Becky rose and rounded the table till she stood staring down at the place setting. But there was no evidence that showed Melanie might have had anything to do with that glass toppling over, like a string or...

"Shit!" Becky shivered, rubbing her hands along her arms. That was entirely too weird, even if she couldn't see how Mel had pulled it off.

Melanie grabbed her napkin and dabbed at the wine before scooping the shards of glass into it. "I don't think Dara agreed with what you said about her death. It wasn't just a stupid thing she did entirely on her own. Somehow, whatever entities are in this house killed her."

Chapter SIXTEEN

WHILE MELANIE CARRIED THE SODDEN NAPKIN and broken glass into the kitchen, Becky sat alone in the giant room watching the flickering flame of the candle. Somehow Melanie had caused that glass to tip over. She didn't know how but that was the only explanation she was willing to believe. A neat trick just like the tricks her eyes were playing on her when she saw the image of a woman in the flash of lightning.

How long was the storm outside going to last? You'd think if it knocked out an electrical tower the power company crews would have it fixed by now. Being at the abandoned resort in the middle of nowhere was bad enough without the lights and electricity failing them too.

This was going to be a long night.

How was she going to stay up keeping vigil if Melanie went to bed? She glanced at her cell phone. Eleven twenty-four. Mel had said she wanted to be awake at midnight when Dara's birthday arrived. She probably had an hour before Mel would turn in and she'd be alone.

In light of some of the things that had happened that evening, that thought wasn't comforting. What would she do to stay awake? There was a book on her cell phone that she could read. It might keep her mind off her surroundings, yet she'd still be able to hear if anyone tried to break in.

When the kitchen door opened and the light flashed from Melanie's cell phone she sat back in her chair, only then aware that she'd been perched on the edge, waiting for something else to happen.

Melanie sat down and fished another joint from the tin pack on the table. "Sure you don't want to try some?"

"Are you kidding? Look how hard it hit Cindy. How are you managing to stay awake when she's out like a light?" Looking at Melanie, there was no way the wisp of a woman should be able to withstand all that wine and weed when Cindy who had a good thirty pounds on Mel had been knocked on her ass.

"I have a high tolerance for THC. I'm only feeling a little buzz." She lit it and then sat back holding the smoke deep in her lungs. When she blew out a plume, she leaned closer to Becky "That freaked you out...that wineglass breaking like that. Dara's not the one we have to worry about though. It's the others."

Becky had just about had enough of all of this talk. She huffed a fast sigh. "*What others*? If you mean the noise we heard earlier that some intruder probably made, then yeah, there's at least one other person on this property besides us."

Melanie's eyes narrowed watching her. "You always were the logical one, weren't you? Well, in this realm you're wrong, Becky. I made a study of this, even starting in university. When you die, it's only the physical body that dies. Who you are, your conscious energy, doesn't stop. Energy can never cease to exist, it just changes."

"This is all based on faith, Melanie. You can't prove any of that. But I know I could talk until I'm blue in the face and you'd never change your belief in this. It's like religions—praying to some magic guy in the sky." She'd had this conversation with lots of people, from atheists to devout church goers. It was kind of a waste of time in the final analysis.

"So premonitions and ESP don't exist according to you. Yet twice in Dara's life she had dreams foretelling an event. But you'd probably explain that as coincidence, right?" Melanie took another long hit off the joint. "I don't want to argue, Becky. All I'm asking is that you try to keep an open mind. For Dara, if not for me."

Becky nodded and glanced across the table to Dara's place setting. "Speaking of Dara, we're almost at the witching hour, Mel."

Melanie glanced at her phone. "Twelve more minutes. She would have been twenty-eight." Still holding the phone, she tapped a few icons and then held the phone out for Becky to see.

A selfie pic of Dara and Melanie, the ocean in the background, filled the small screen. Becky reached for the phone and expanded the photo of the two friends. They were polar opposites, Melanie's pale, wheat-colored hair and ivory complexion next to Dara's dark locks and Mediterranean-toned skin. And typical of their personalities, Melanie's smile was shy while Dara flaunted her good looks.

Melanie reached for the phone, explaining the photo. "That was when she came to visit me. I never dreamed it would be the last time I'd see her alive." She set the phone in the center of the table leaving the photo showing.

"You said you tried a séance to contact her father. Was that her idea or yours, Mel?"

"Believe it or not, it was Dara's. She cried herself to sleep when we were unable to make contact. I think she took it as him rejecting her once more. I think that's why she sunk her teeth into this place, like a dog with a bone. She wanted to prove to him she could do it."

"But Dara had always been successful in her investments. She surely didn't need to prove anything, especially to her dead father. The guy must have been terribly demanding." It was funny. She'd always been a little envious of Dara's wealth and lifestyle, yet Dara had never really been happy from the sounds of it.

THUD! SMASH!

Becky jerked ramrod stiff in her seat. It came from the kitchen!

The whites of Melanie's eyes could be seen when she peered over at Becky. "It's them! They don't want us here."

Hardly daring to breathe, Becky slowly rose to her feet. Her hand slipped behind her grabbing the gun from her jeans. "It's that intruder, Mel. He must have a key to the kitchen door."

She held the gun with shaking hands, inching her way across the room to the kitchen. Shit! Why had she ever agreed to come here? Plus, she didn't know *anything* about guns. Was there a safety that needed to be flipped so it could work?

"You've got a gun too? For God's sake, Becky! That's not going to help you here!" Melanie was on her feet, brushing past Becky. "Don't shoot me or anything. Actually, put that stupid thing away!"

Melanie held the cell phone high, pushing the door open with her foot. Becky lowered the gun at her side the way Cindy had done. Melanie was taking charge, but if there was some thug in there, she made up her mind to shoot first and ask questions later.

"Holy shit!" Melanie turned to look at her before disappearing inside the kitchen. Becky hurried after her, following the beam of light from Melanie's phone.

Every drawer in the lower cabinets was yanked out. The top one, laying on the floor was turned upside down with cutlery scattered near it.

"Check the door, Melanie!"

Melanie shone the light over there, but it was closed, and the dead bolt was still set in place. She did a quick scan of the room with the light before returning to the gaping drawers.

In that sweep of light, there'd been no person lurking in the room, about to attack them. It was just the two of them there. Becky's heart thundered so hard that she swore Melanie must be able to hear it. Finally, she managed to get the words out, "How? Who did this?"

Melanie shone the light on the floor. Silver knives and spoons glinted in the blue glare of the beam. "*What* did this, is more like it. It's the same forces that drove Dara into the lake. This is a warning to us, Becky. They want us gone from this place."

Working her way down the cupboards, Melanie pushed the drawers that hung open, back into their slots. She grabbed the drawer from the floor and slid it into its spot. Scooping up the cutlery, she placed the items in the sink.

Becky was frozen in place watching Melanie be so efficient and matter of fact. This couldn't be happening. Drawers didn't just fly open by themselves, with enough force that one had landed on the floor. Yet there was no one here.

"What should we do?" Becky grabbed Melanie's arm, yanking her close and peering into her eyes.

Melanie sighed. "We can't leave if that's what you're getting at. We can't abandon Dara."

Becky didn't know about abandoning Dara but she did know if they left, they'd be abandoning the inheritance. That would be a reckless thing to do. There'd been some creepy things happening since they arrived but nothing that threatened them physically. Yet.

There was one full day and one more night to get through. If they stuck together, they could do it. Cindy would agree with that reasoning.

She took a deep breath to settle her nerves "No. We're not leaving, Mel. Don't worry." Her chin rose higher, defiantly proclaiming, "Today is Dara's birthday. Happy birthday, Dara."

Mel nodded. "Yeah. Happy birthday, my friend. We're here for you." She turned and walked over to the cabinet over the stove. She plucked a box from the shelf and held it in her hand.

Becky looked at the box. "What's with the salt?"

"Protection." Melanie's gaze shifted to the gun that Becky still held with a shaking hand. "It's a damn sight more useful with what we're up against than that gun." She jerked her head, signaling for Becky to go back into the reception room.

Becky was only too happy to leave the kitchen. She stepped into the room and watched Melanie pour a line of salt across the door opening.

"From everything I've read, salt is one thing that evil spirits abhor. We'll see how well it works for us. I think we should pour a line across the entrance to where our rooms are." Melanie straightened and walked over to that doorway.

Becky's breath froze in her chest. The thought of staying up, alone, in the large reception room filled her with dread. "Are you going to bed now? How can you sleep after...after—"

"After the 'no such thing as ghosts' sent a nasty warning shot?" Even in the low light from the cell phone, a smirk was visible on Melanie's face. She finished setting the line of salt across the entryway to the wing where their rooms were. "Cindy's in there. We need to protect her too. I'm finishing my glass of wine in tribute to Dara and then I'm going to bed."

Becky went over to the candle's light and took her seat at the table. That thing in the kitchen had shaken her. She couldn't deny it. There might be a plausible explanation for it, but right then, sitting in a dark room at midnight, the explanation that Melanie had suggested kept bouncing around in her brain.

Damn it. Her gaze lowered to her hands. She should stay up and keep an eye out for that intruder. But what if there wasn't anyone out there? If Melanie was right, she'd be sitting here alone facing the specter of more creepy things happening. And why did she have to stand guard in the reception room full of shadows?

She nodded coming to a decision. She could force herself to stay awake and alert in the relative safety of her own room. No way was she staying out here after all that had happened.

She looked at Melanie as she took a seat at the table. "I'm tired too. But I'll keep you company while you finish your wine."

Melanie's face twisted in a sneer. "Yeah right. Still think there's no afterlife, no God or anything after you die?"

She could feel her cheeks grow warmer being caught out by Mel. The old Mel was more likeable than this new improved version. New Mel is assertive; Old Mel was a mouse. The old Mel would never be so forthright or critical.

Becky forced a smile. "I'm not ruling out that there could be a logical explanation for what happened in the kitchen. We don't know what that lawyer may have done to the house before we were summoned here. He may have set booby traps to scare us away."

Mel finished her wine and set the glass down. "Dara was his *friend* as well as client. She wouldn't have used him if she felt he couldn't be trusted. I didn't get any bad vibes from the guy. I think you two have a hard time trusting anyone, especially with this much money on the line."

Becky had had it with Mel's superior attitude. "So the money means nothing to you? You'd be here if she hadn't left us a penny. Is that what you expect me to believe?"

"I don't expect you or Cindy to understand my motives. Furthermore, I don't really care if you don't." She sighed as she got to her feet, clicking the flashlight app on. "Blow the candle out before you go to bed, will you? I'm done in for today."

Immediately Becky regretted her outburst. "Look, I'm sorry, Mel. Dara was a friend to all of us. We need to stick together to get through this weekend and honor her memory."

Mel paused, and her shoulders slumped a little when she looked back at Becky. "You still don't get it. We're not just honoring Dara; we're going to set her free. If we can." She turned and continued walking across the room while Becky doused the candle.

Chapter SEVENTEEN

BECKY SAID GOODNIGHT to Melanie and entered her room. Stopping at the threshold, she flashed the beam from her cell phone across the room, examining it for any sign of an intruder or other crazy stuff. The sprig of jasmine still lay on her pillow where she'd last seen it. A glance at the face of the phone showed that it was now twelve fifty-three.

Just two more hours until she could wake Cindy to take over this vigil. Two hours to stay awake in relative peace and quiet with any luck.

She went into the bathroom but left the door open behind her. Every sense in her body was on high alert, listening, trying to see through the darkness for any movement. But the only sounds were the rain and wind outside. With the low focus of the phone's light, she couldn't see into the dark corners of the room.

She finished her nightly ritual by splashing cold water on her face and neck. A glance in the mirror showed shadows under her eyes and a worn gauntness that hadn't been there that morning. Her body was bone-tired but thoughts in her head kept pinging, like she'd drank ten cups of coffee.

To make matters worse, Hank hadn't bothered to call even though she'd left a message. Nice of him to care so much. He'd been so distant the past six months, *saying* that his research was having problems. She smiled to herself. That was going to change when this was all over, wouldn't it?

She left the bathroom and then settled on the bed, propping her back against the headboard. She was being childish and vindictive. He was probably up to his elbows in research forgetting the world around him. He probably hadn't even stopped to eat. It wouldn't be the first time. That had to be it.

A flash of lightning lit the room, making her jerk back. The thunder that followed after a couple seconds let her know that the storm hadn't passed...or maybe a new one had rolled in. She scrolled through the apps on her phone, searching for the book that she'd started a few nights ago. A glance at the battery icon showed that the power left was on the halfway mark. With another five hours till daylight, she might need that power. So much for reading.

She got up and wandered over to the window, gazing out at the dark night. Watching the storm with the bursts of lightning would kill some time. At least she'd be on her feet and not tempted to drift off. Not that she could anyway after that crap in the kitchen. How the hell had that happened?

And what about the lipstick on the glass? It had been *etched* in, not smeared.

Oh God. And that woman who had appeared in the flash of lightning. She could still see her, and there was no denying that it had looked like Dara. Too many things had happened that defied her powers of logic.

A burst of lightning in the distance showed the lake against a backdrop of dark mountains. She stepped back bracing for the clap of thunder that was sure to follow. Even so, she jumped when it boomed above. The wind hurtled rain droplets hard as hail against the glass while another flash broke the darkness.

In that burst of light, she'd seen movement, a dark shadow caught in the glare. There was someone on the balcony to the left of her! She peered hard over at the area, hoping for another flare of the storm. But of course, when she wanted it to happen, it stayed black as tar. She'd seen it though. In that fraction of a second it was hard to tell if it was a man or a woman.

She hurried back to the bed, tucking the pillow into her chest like a shield. There was nothing she could accomplish watching the outside. There was no way on earth she was going out there, even with the gun in her hand. And if it was some entity, even Dara's essence, she wasn't going to face it alone. She huddled against the headboard, trying to get her breathing under control and think this through.

Should she wake Cindy? Cindy would be a voice of reason against all the superstition that Melanie had spouted. And at that hour of the night reason was the only thing that could keep her sane.

This must have been what it was like for Dara. But Dara had been alone. Maybe she'd run screaming to the lake to get away from this resort. It *had* been at night that she'd drowned. Why would she stay here by herself? Had she been so driven by a need to please her father that she'd put herself at risk? Hell, she'd even had a premonition of her death. Crazy.

Melanie was convinced Dara was trapped here still. Convinced that she'd arranged this horrible weekend to enlist their help. Becky looked around the room even though she couldn't see anything, now that she'd turned the cell phone off. "Dara. If Mel's right and you're here, how can we help you? What do you want?"

A tap on her bedroom door almost caused Becky's heart to stop! Oh God! Dara?

"Becky? Open up."

She breathed a sigh of relief hearing Cindy's voice. She flicked the phone on and rushed to the door to open it. Cindy stood there with wide eyes, rubbing her hands over her upper arms.

"Something woke me up. You came in and shook me, right?" She reached out and gripped Becky's arms in a death grip. "It was you, right?"

Becky shook her head slowly, feeling her stomach tighten with dread. "No. It wasn't me." The look on Cindy's face, her eyes darting back over her shoulder told her that she was rattled as well.

She stepped inside, brushing past Becky, "I was out cold, you know. But someone shook my shoulder and said my name."

Even though Becky had her doubts, she had to put it out there. "Maybe Mel? Maybe she woke you. We should—"

"It wasn't Mel. I was going out to the reception room to get you, and I heard her snoring in her room. Remember? She could wake the dead. I don't know how Dara..." She stopped and patted the back of her pants. "My gun! Where the hell's my gun?"

Becky reached around and then handed the gun to Cindy. "Sorry. I took it. I figured it wouldn't do us any good if you had it and you were passed out."

"You're supposed to be in the reception area keeping guard. Instead, you're in here probably falling asleep! Someone got in here, Becky, and *touched me*." Cindy held the gun before her about to leave the room again to find the intruder.

"Wait." Becky grabbed Cindy's arm. "Something happened in the kitchen around midnight." She watched Cindy's eyes narrow. "All the drawers in the cabinets suddenly flew wide open all by themselves. I checked for anyone breaking in, but the dead bolt was still set and the kitchen was empty. Melanie thought it was the ghosts in this house trying to warn us."

"Will you *listen* to yourself, Becky! I leave you for a couple hours alone with that nut job, and she's got you believing this shit. Come on! We need to catch the bastard who woke me up."

"Stop!" Becky's hands flew in the air, accidentally shining the light full on in Cindy's eyes. "Sorry. The voice...was it a woman's or a man's voice?"

Cindy sighed, but her chin dropped as she tried to recall. "I don't know. It was a whisper. A *loud* whisper. Why does that matter, anyway?"

Becky's forehead knotted trying to think her way through this. "It doesn't matter, I guess." She risked a peek at Cindy. "Unless, it was Dara. I think I saw her earlier in the reception room before dinner."

"What? Why didn't you tell me? Are you sure you saw her and not some trick of the light? Dara is *dead*, Becky. You're starting to scare me.

This kind of talk is more Melanie than you." Cindy edged back shaking her head slightly.

"I know how this sounds, okay? But in a flash of lightning, I saw a woman sitting in Dara's spot." Becky was coiled tight, waiting for Cindy to lay into her the way she'd laid into Mel.

"No. Come on, Becky. Not you too. Bad enough I have Melanie acting all weird. But you?" Cindy's face fell, and she looked at the floor.

"At first, I thought it was an afterimage, something the glare of lightning created. But after the kitchen drawers slammed open, I'm not so sure." She saw Cindy's face grow even tighter, and blurted, "Dara's wineglass fell over and broke. There's no way Melanie or me caused that. It just tipped all on its own."

Cindy was silent for a few moments examining Becky's face. "Jesus Becky. I can see it upset you. It's creepy as hell. Even I have to admit that. But Becky, let's not rule out the fact that there may be a real person here who is trying to scare us off. We need to check the kitchen and the other doors." She stepped out of the room and then stopped, looking back at Becky. "Well? Are you coming with me or not?"

Becky's gut was a twisted knot at the thought of going back out there. But she couldn't let Cindy face it alone. She almost wished that Cindy was right. It'd be easier to face a real person than what Melanie had proposed, what she'd seen with her own eyes. "Yes. We should stick together."

When they passed Melanie's room, she could hear the woman's snores, passed out, sawing logs like a lumberjack. Hard to believe such a petite person could make that racket and not wake up. Mel claimed it was because of a deviated septum in her nose. She should get that fixed with the money she was inheriting. The sleep clinic Mel had gone to sure hadn't helped her.

Cindy held the gun in one hand and her cell phone in the other lighting the way. When they got to the reception area, the first thing she did was check the two doors that she'd nailed shut. Becky could see that everything was just the way they'd left it.

"That's good. But I'm pretty sure we would have heard a racket if they tried to get in that way." Cindy paused flashing the light at the table where the half-empty wine and glasses still sat. "Bring one of those chairs into the kitchen will you, Becky?"

Becky lifted the chair and followed Cindy into the kitchen. She wasn't sure if she should tell Cindy about the line of salt that spread over the entryway. She'd probably just get angry again so she let it pass. Even so, Becky stepped higher, trying hard to not disturb it.

Cindy waved the light over the whole room before shining the beam on the door to the outside. "Wedge the back of that chair under the handle, Becky. If someone is around and they have a key, that will stop them."

Becky stepped by the counter and the drawers that had flown open earlier. She'd have a closer look at that in the light of day to see if there was some gadget rigged up to make them fly open. Hopefully there would be.

"Where'd you learn this trick with the chair? Your cop friend?"

Cindy snorted. "I have two older brothers, remember? This saved me on more than one occasion. They were always playing tricks on me, driving me nuts." She walked over to the drawers under the countertop and tugged the top one out.

Becky checked the chair again, making sure it would stay in place before joining Cindy. "That drawer landed on the floor. The cutlery is in the sink."

"Weird." Cindy led the way back into the reception area. She shone the light once more over the room and then at the window next to the front entry. "Set another chair under the front door's knob for good measure."

Even though Becky was dog-tired, she did as Cindy asked. She wedged it in tight and then turned to her friend. "Are you staying out here? I don't think that's—"

"Yes. I'll be here until sunup. I may wake you then and go back to bed to catch a few more hours of sleep." Cindy pulled a chair out and sat down heavily.

There was something niggling in the back of Becky's mind the whole time she'd followed Cindy out to check on things. It suddenly popped up like an air bubble swirling to the surface in a lake.

"Did you check your bedroom for water droplets on the floor, Cindy? If there *is* someone else here and they went into your room to wake you, they would have been out in the storm. There should be water from their feet."

Cindy rose to her feet. "Shit. You're right. I never thought of that. Let's go."

She walked quickly, and Becky had to almost run to keep up. She slowed when they entered Cindy's room, her gaze following the cone of light that Cindy aimed at the floor from the entryway over to the bed. The wooden floor was bone dry, but there was a dark reddish spot next to the night table. Cindy bent over, and when she straightened there was a red rose petal in her hand.

Chapter EIGHTEEN

A SHIVER OF FEAR SKITTERED through Becky's shoulders seeing the petal in Cindy's hand. Dara. The voice and even shaking Cindy to wake her, had been their deceased friend. And she'd left a calling card to make sure they knew it was her.

"Dara. She's the one who whispered in your ear, Cindy. She's here." Becky stared at Cindy trying to see if this was registering with her.

"No. That can't be. I felt a real hand on my shoulder, shaking me until I woke." Cindy flicked the petal away from her fingertips. "That petal could have stuck to my sneaker and fell off." She was silent a few moments, staring at the rose petal on the floor. "It had to be Melanie. She moves like a cat."

It sounded crazy even to her own ears, yet...

"But she's sound asleep, Cindy." Becky's words were lost on Cindy as she stepped by her, once more leading with the beam of light.

She stopped at Melanie's door, listening. A nasally snort was followed once more by the rhythmic rumble of Melanie snoring. She turned the handle of the door and eased it open. Becky followed her creeping over to the bed where a mound of bedcovers bunched around their friend.

Cindy's hand drifted forward to tug at the comforter, checking to see that Melanie was indeed asleep. When her fingers lifted the coverlet, only a pillow showed. Pulling it higher revealed another couple of pillows shaped to look like a person.

"What the hell?"

All the while the sound of Melanie's snoring droned in the air around them. Cindy lifted the pillow and sure enough the light of a cell phone flared in their eyes. The snoring was coming from that! She'd recorded her own sleep and was playing it! But where was she?

"Why would she *do* that?" Becky's mouth fell open, her gaze flitting from the bed to Cindy's face.

"I told you she was going to pull something. That was why you were supposed to watch her as well as the doors. I guess we know who woke me up." Cindy clicked a button on Mel's phone and the snoring stopped. She pocketed the phone in her jeans.

Becky shook her head slowly. "She's obsessed. Now I'm not sure if she didn't have something to do with what happened in the kitchen earlier. Or even if the power is really off."

Cindy nodded. "We're on the same page now, Becky. We don't know if this is actually Mel's first time at the resort, do we? She could have come up here last week and set this up so that strange things happen. She may even have some kind of remote control to douse the lights, and send the drawers flying across the room."

Becky's jaw twitched and she clenched her teeth. "It's a hell of a lot of money involved with Dara's will." She shook her head sadly. "Mel says the money's not important but how do we know that? Anyone who would rig up her bed to make us think she's here while all the while she's out sneaking around, isn't someone we can really trust."

Cindy sighed. "We were close friends in university but people change. Hell, we only see each other once a year. It's not hard to act like everything's cool when it's just for a few days." When Cindy looked at Becky, there was a hard glint in her eyes. "Maybe she was involved with Dara's death. She could have been here. We only have her word that she wasn't."

Becky stepped closer to Cindy, whispering, "We checked the doors, checked the kitchen and reception area. Where is she?"

At the series of loud thuds both women jerked back.

Becky clutched at Cindy's arm. "What was that?"

Again, the thuds thundered around them, even louder this time.

"It's coming from the reception area. The door? Someone's at the door!" Cindy once more grabbed her gun from the back of her jeans.

"It's got to be Mel! She must have gone outside and now she can't get in." Becky followed Cindy out of the room and down the hallway.

Cindy called over her shoulder as she entered the reception area. "I'm not taking any chances." She held the gun before her, aiming it at the door. "Who's there?"

"It's me, Melanie! Let me in!"

Becky stepped by Cindy and lifted the chair from where she'd wedged it under the door handle. She went to flip the dead bolt lock off but it was already off. Shit. She should have checked that earlier. When she opened the door, she stepped back getting out of the line of fire from the gun.

Melanie stood there in soaking wet pajamas, her pale hair plastered to her head and hanging in strings. A droplet of water fell from her chin. "What the heck? You're going to shoot me, Cindy? Put that gun down, right now." She strode into the room, shutting the door behind her and setting the dead bolt.

"What were you doing out there? And what's with rigging your room to make us think you were sleeping in there? You got some explaining to do, Mel." Cindy lowered the gun but still held it using both hands, ready at a moment's notice.

Melanie rolled her eyes and then bunched and squeezed her hair, ringing a stream of water onto the floor. "I didn't want you to worry about me. I knew you'd be checking up on me, so I made it so you'd think I was asleep. You two would never understand in a million years what's going on in this place. Plus, you think I'm slightly crazy to start with."

"Slightly? Melanie, I'm a therapist, and I can certify you as totally bonkers. Why would you trick us, and what the hell were you doing out in the middle of a thunderstorm?" Becky shook her head watching her friend who looked like a drowned rat.

"I've got to get changed. Thanks to you two bolting the door with the chair, I'm totally soaked. I woke up thinking of Dara." Her head tilted to the side, staring at the floor. "Actually, I heard her voice. At first, I thought I was dreaming, but she touched my shoulder and I could smell roses. I got up and for some reason went out into the storm to be at the lake."

Cindy's voice had risen, and it was clear she wasn't buying Mel's explanation. "We all agreed to stay inside the lodge! I had secured all the entries. You promised, Mel. You put yourself and us in danger by going out there."

Mel replied in a dreamy voice and a faraway look in her eyes. "It was like I was in a trance, slipping out of the lodge and walking to the lake. The water looked so dark and cold. I miss her so much. At a clap of thunder, I sort of came to and ran back up here. Not that you two believe me." Melanie looked over at Cindy. "Mind shining the light or give the phone to Becky so she can? I've got to get out of these wet clothes."

Becky grabbed the phone from Cindy's pocket and shone it on the entrance to their wing. She followed Mel's wet footprints all the way into the woman's bedroom.

Cindy stepped in line beside her. "Wait a minute, Mel. You had this all planned out. You even brought a recording of your sleep. Who *does* that kind of thing? What else have you been up to?"

When they stepped into the room, Melanie rummaged through her suitcase trying to find dry clothes. Becky held the cell phone slightly away to give Mel some privacy to change out of the wet things.

"First of all, I haven't been up to anything. I'm here the same as you to honor Dara's will. But unlike you two pigheaded jerks, I *know* Dara's spirit is still here. As for the recording of my sleep...it was on my phone already. I just turned it on to get you two to leave me alone." She turned to Becky. "You remember, my sleep apnea? I contacted you about the sleep clinic I was going to. They suggested I record my sleep before I come in."

Becky nodded. "Yes. I remember that." She looked over at Cindy who was still watching Mel with narrow eyes. "We exchanged a couple of emails about it."

"Bullshit. You came into my room, Mel, to wake me up. Don't lie. You're prowling around here doing everything you can to scare us. You want the money for yourself." Cindy stepped closer to Mel. "I don't buy this sleep apnea crap. It's just too convenient."

Melanie rolled her eyes. "You're so cynical. I woke up when Dara whispered in my ear. At first, I thought she was asking for my help but she repeated it. 'I'm going to help you, hon.' And then I felt the need to go to the spot where she drowned."

Cindy's head jerked back like she had been slapped. Her eyes spanned wide, and mouth fell open, looking totally horrified. Reaching out, her fingers dug into Becky's arm. Cindy's voice cracked as she stared at Melanie. "What? She said she was going to help you? She used the word, 'hon'?"

"Yeah. Which is weird because it's Dara who needs our help." Melanie's eyes narrowed at Cindy. "I get it. She came to you too. She said the exact words, didn't she?"

"Same words." Cindy let out a huff of air as she gave her head a shake. "But I'm still not convinced it was Dara. It makes me suspect you even more."

All the while Becky stood watching the exchange, not sure which version to believe. But if it was Dara offering help to Melanie and Cindy, why had she been excluded? Something wasn't adding up but she was entirely too worn out to figure it out now.

She was sick of the bickering, sick of the resort and ready to shut everything out for some sleep. It was now almost two thirty in the morning. She looked at Cindy and Melanie. "I'm going to bed." She started walking out of Melanie's room, but Cindy's voice stopped her.

"I vote we all stay together in one room. I'll stay up and keep watch while you and Melanie try to get some sleep." Cindy walked over to the upholstered chair near the window and plopped down in it.

"Who made you the boss? Maybe I don't want you in my room." Melanie folded her arms over her chest, glaring at Cindy.

Becky's jaw tightened. "Just cut it out, will you? Cindy's right. There's been weird things happening around here and until we figure this out, we need to watch each other's back." Becky rounded the bed and grabbed the pillows from where Melanie had staged them in the center of the bed. She yanked the coverlet back and got in.

"Fine." Melanie rooted in her suitcase, shining the cell's light into it. When her hand emerged, she had a small plastic case.

Becky watched her open it and then pop what looked like a dental retainer into her mouth. With any luck it would stop Mel's snoring and let her get a good night's sleep. She rolled over, feeling the bed depress when Melanie got in the other side.

But sleep was a long time coming.

Chapter NINETEEN

THE SOUNDS OF BIRDS CHIRPING outside gradually seeped into Becky's consciousness as she huddled under the down comforter. It was so cozy and warm in the nest she'd made she hesitated in creaking an eye open. Daylight filled the window, pouring past Cindy curled up like a cat in the easy chair, sound asleep.

She pushed herself up from the pillow and turned to look at Melanie. When she saw the empty spot, she grimaced. A glance at the bathroom showed the door ajar, the room behind it dark and empty. Tossing back the comforter she sat up and pushed her feet into her sneakers.

Melanie was probably up making breakfast. She tiptoed by Cindy and shut the door, leaving her friend fast asleep. The fact that she was sleeping was a good sign. The rest of the night must have passed in relative peace, so much so that she finally drifted off.

She wandered down the hallway and out into the large reception area. The front door was wide open and Melanie stood on the front step, sipping from a steaming mug.

Melanie didn't even turn around when she called to Becky, "Coffee's made. Grab a cup and come join me. We need to talk."

"So, the power's back on?"

"Yes."

Becky's eyes closed and she sighed continuing on into the kitchen. The smell of coffee was a much more welcoming greeting than Melanie had shown her. She grabbed a mug and was about to pour a cup when she noticed at the far end of the room, the door gaping wide to the outside. The chair that she'd wedged under the handle was set off to the side.

Damn it. Melanie wasn't taking the threat that there might be an intruder seriously enough. She set the mug down and went over to the door. She was about to shut it but on second thought she stepped outside, examining the overgrown and broken flagstone patio for anything suspicious.

Weeds crowded out what was probably at one time a raised bed of herbs at the edge of the open area. Beyond that a pathway tried to wind its way through enormously mature, old maple and oak trees. Their trunks had to be at least four feet or more in diameter. On the other side the three-story wing of the resort loomed, the broken windows looking like the multifaceted eyes of an insect peering down at her.

She shuddered at the thought of being watched. Retreating back into the kitchen, she locked the door, and once more wedged the chair for added security. She finished fixing the coffee with cream and sugar and went out to join Melanie at the front entry. But Melanie had left the front steps and now stood on the circular balcony overlooking the garden and lake.

The balcony might once have boasted a gorgeous view of the greenery and water but now it looked like it was ready to topple over. The railing was missing many spindles and had pulled away from the thick upper supports in a few spots. When Becky stepped onto the balcony, wooden planks gave a little, water seeping from them with each step she took. Moss had taken hold in the crevices and clung to the corners everywhere she looked.

A glance at Mel showed her jaw set and eyes peering hard at the lake. She was probably still teed off about being locked out and then Cindy not believing her. Becky decided to try to lighten the mood. "I never heard you snore once last night. That appliance sure works. I think that sleep clinic—"

"Today is Dara's birthday. We need to help her."

Becky had a hard time stopping the roll of her eyes, but she managed to keep her voice steady. "You keep saying that, Mel. How do you propose we actually *do* that?" She'd had way too little sleep to put up with Mel's cryptic comments.

Melanie turned to face her. "We do a séance tonight. I brought everything we'll need."

Becky snorted. "That explains the candle you produced out of thin air. I mean who in hell travels with a candle in their bag?" She took a long sip of coffee, savoring the sweetness. "Cindy will never go along with this. I'm not sure I want to either. Even you have to admit that last night was unsettling."

"Of course, it was. There's nothing the spirits who reside here want more than for us to leave. But that's exactly why we need to confront them. Dara needs us to." Melanie's voice was flat and matter of fact, brooking no argument. "She'll be her strongest tonight."

"What the hell do you mean?"

"Not only is it the night of Dara's birthday, but it's also the Autumn Equinox."

"What, Fall begins tonight and that's a big deal?"

"Yes. Spirits are strongest on the night of the equinoxes." She held out both her hands. "During an equinox the Moon and Earth are in balance. And because of that, it's when the spirit world and our world are in perfect balance." She chewed her lower lip for a moment. "Things can slip through the barrier easier. Having a séance could give Dara extra help to contact us. Our presence supporting her can open the door."

"Open the door, huh?" Becky's voice was icy. "Speaking of doors, why did you leave the kitchen door open, Mel? You expect us to buy into all this spiritual crap but you don't respect our opinion that there might be an intruder trying to scare us."

"I *know* there's no intruder. *We're* the intruders. The sooner you and Cindy get on board with that, the safer we'll be." Her voice broke, fighting back tears. "You need to put aside your preconceived ideas and help in contacting Dara."

Becky's grip on her mug grew tighter and she scowled at Melanie. "According to you and Cindy, Dara offered to help *you*. If I can actually believe that. Odd that Cindy and you both heard the same words at around the same time last night."

Melanie's head fell back and she snorted. "Oh my God. You're actually jealous that you weren't included in that. For a skeptic that's pretty rich!"

"I'm not *jealous*. Suspicious, but certainly not jealous." Becky felt her cheeks get warmer being caught out by Melanie. This wasn't the way things normally happened. Melanie was entirely too high and mighty these days. To say nothing of delusional and...greedy?

"Hey!"

They both turned at Cindy's voice. Cindy was on the front step carrying a mug of coffee over to join them.

"What are you two arguing about? You should have woke me up. I thought we were going to stick together like glue from now on." She looked like a refugee, wearing the blanket that had covered her the night before over her shoulders.

Becky spoke before Melanie had a chance. "You'd better get Mel on board with that. She was up way before us, opening the back door of the kitchen for anyone to enter. And *coincidentally* the electricity is back on."

"Oh. I see." Cindy exchanged a look with Becky. Quick as anything, she turned on Becky. "What about you? You didn't try to wake me."

Becky had had enough of their criticism. "Sue me for being kind. I thought you could use some extra sleep after staying up most of the night. Or did you pass out like us?"

Cindy took a deep breath, pausing a few beats before she answered. "I saw the first light of day and then I fell asleep."

Melanie finished her mug of coffee and then turned to them. "I'm getting another cup of coffee...or am I allowed to go to the kitchen on my own?" Sarcasm dripped off her tongue.

"I don't know about you, but it's not all that pleasant standing out on this thing." Cindy tested the railing, pushing it out about a foot while it creaked ominously. "Let's all go in and get breakfast ready."

Becky didn't have to be asked twice to leave the decrepit structure. She hurried after Melanie and Cindy, shutting the door behind her. The day was overcast and damp, a leftover from the storm the night before.

When she stepped into the kitchen she almost stepped into Cindy. "What the hell?"

Becky's breath hitched in her chest when she managed to get by Cindy. Oh my God. The chair that she'd propped under the doorknob was now halfway up the wall next to it. How? She followed Melanie over, her eyes examining the wall for a hook or nail, anything that was holding the chair suspended.

Cindy's voice was soft with wonder. "How did that chair get up there? It wasn't like that when I came in for coffee. And we were—"

"It's *them*. They did this to send a message." Melanie hissed and then turned to reach for the leg of the chair.

The hair on the back of Becky's neck spiked higher as she watched the suspended object. This couldn't be happening. There was no hook or any physical reason for that chair to be up there. Even when Melanie gave the chair leg a good tug it only wiggled a bit. A quick dart of her gaze to the dead bolt showed it still latched.

Crash! The chair bounced onto the floor.

She jerked back, her hand flying to her throat. What the hell? She looked at the chair and the wall with eyes that were almost popped out onto her cheekbones. That couldn't have happened. But...it did.

"Holy shit!" Cindy stepped closer but avoided touching it.

Melanie looked at both of them. "Now do you see? There's a presence here that wants us to leave. It's trying to frighten us. And it's definitely not some thug hired by that lawyer."

Cindy was pale and shaking when she spoke. "But...we have to tell him! This changes everything. If he isn't in on this, and it's beginning to look like he isn't, then there's no way we can stay here. He wouldn't expect us to, if he knew."

Melanie turned on Cindy, nearly shouting in her face. "He knows! He knows that Dara's death wasn't an accident! You may not have picked up on it, but he couldn't get out of here fast enough. He felt it too. So no. He's not about to help us with this."

Becky finally recovered enough from the shock that she was able to speak. "Wait a minute. You don't know that for sure. I'm with Cindy. We have to try to contact him. You were the one who took his card, not Cindy. Hand it over, Melanie. No more screwing around."

Melanie looked like she was about to tear her hair out, practically yelling when she answered, "I don't have his card! You seriously think that something that can levitate a chair, yank out every drawer is unable to hide a damn business card? Get real."

Cindy looked like a caged animal, her eyes darting around the room. "Oh God. What if she's telling the truth."

But Becky wasn't giving up so easily. "I know his first name is Anthony and he works in Watertown. We can do an internet search for lawyers. Call everyone with Anthony as the first name." She took a few steps toward the door leading to the reception area and stopped. "Well? Come on! We need our cell phones."

"Good thinking. We can plug them in to recharge at the same time." Cindy was right on Becky's tail while Melanie muttered how useless this was...a total waste of time.

Becky ignored Mel. A call to the lawyer was definitely in order. Considering he was supposed to be there the next afternoon, he might still be in the area. Things were getting too creepy and out of control to handle this by themselves. She marched into Melanie's room and over to the bedside table where she'd left the phone.

It lay in pieces. Not just the screen splintered but the back torn off and the tiny wires and gizmos blackened like they'd been nuked.

Behind her, Cindy's voice said, "Oh my God."

At Cindy's shocked whisper, Becky turned to see her holding the parts of her phone. A glance at Melanie showed the same. They were stuck there without a way to contact the outside world.

No. Not stuck. They still had the car outside.

Cindy looked over at Becky, "You know, that money isn't going to do any of us any good if we're dead. Whatever is playing with us means business. I vote we leave."

Melanie put her hand up, "No! We stay. Dara needs our help. We can do this."

They both looked over at Becky.

There had to be another way. Leaving would mean losing the money to say nothing of Dara's last request of them. But Cindy had a point. This *thing* or *things* could move furniture and had even obliterated their cell phones.

"Is there anything we can do to protect ourselves, Melanie?"

Melanie blurted, "Salt. We have salt."

"That's it? And what about the thing you claim Dara said to you, that she'd help us? I'm trying to make a case for staying, but Cindy has a good point too. I'm scared." And it was true. Becky's legs felt like they'd give out any second and her hands shook. She wasn't sure how much more she could take of this stuff.

"Dara will help us. And in turn we will help free her. You have to have faith, Becky." Melanie stepped over, and her hands clasped Becky's shoulders, pleading with her eyes as well as her words.

Becky took a deep breath. Somehow, they had to stay and finish this for Dara as well as for themselves. God only knew how generous Dara had been to them. And still was.

Cindy threw her hands in the air, grinding her teeth before she spoke. "Will you listen to yourself?" She stepped over to Becky. "Where are the car keys? If you two want to stay that's your business. I'm not that hard up that I want to risk my life."

Becky jerked back. "You'd actually leave us here? What happened to friendship? Looking out for one another? But considering your history, you always looked out for number one, didn't you?"

Melanie weighed in too. "Yeah. You never really liked Dara. You were always trying to get one up on her, any way you could."

Cindy's eyes narrowed, her gaze flitting between Becky and Mel. "You guys don't have a clue. If not for me, Dara would have been disowned by her father. Which all things considered might have been for the best. At least she'd be alive."

"What are you talking about? She would have told me if there'd been a serious problem. She confided in me about *everything*." Melanie folded her arms across her chest challenging Cindy.

"Oh yeah? I'm sure she talked to an airhead like you about investments. Yeah, right."

Becky's jaw dropped. What was this talk of investments all about? Cindy didn't have to be so cruel to Melanie either.

But this was the new Mel who wasn't about to back down. "Yeah, right. You expect us to believe she talked to you about money? Sought the advice of a working-class kid for her *investment* acumen? That's equally implausible."

Cindy's eyes narrowed. "Just because I never had money didn't mean I was ignorant about investing. Remember? I took that finance course, and we were talking about Ponzi schemes. Shortly after, I was looking for something on Dara's desk, a pen or something, when I came across those letters from an investment firm."

"You snooped into her private affairs?" Melanie screeched. "I knew it. I knew she didn't confide in you. You're a sneaky liar. Just like the time you were caught plagiarizing—"

"No, you twit! I wasn't snooping! The name on the letterhead rang a bell. I'd heard it before. She was investing most of her monthly income from her grandmother's trust. Getting astronomical returns, like thirty to forty percent!"

"Tell me where to sign up. That's crazy. The most I've ever gotten was seven on some Asian equity fund." Becky sank down on the bed, eager to hear more.

"Well, that's just it! No one gets that kind of return! Too good to be true? I'll say. I called my brother's friend who had a job in the Securities Exchange Commission. I told him the name of the firm. He didn't name names, but he told me to stay clear of them. I took that to mean the company was under investigation."

"So, you told Dara?"

Cindy's fingers threaded through her hair, and then fisted like she was at her wit's end. "Will you let me finish, Mel? Dara was only a few months away from inheriting her mother's estate. She was going to invest that with this outfit. That's what they really wanted." She snapped her fingers. "Stanford Finance. That was the outfit. They were trying to get their hands on that money. She would have lost it all, and her father would have disowned her."

Melanie tsked. "You don't know that for sure."

"Yes I do! It was only six months after that that I learned they'd been arrested. I saw my brother's friend Eric at Christmas break and he told me. Lucky for Dara that I was able to steer her away before she gave them that chunk of money." Her face fell a little, looking at the floor. "It was between Dara and me—our secret. We may have competed on grades and boyfriends, superficial stuff, but we had each other's back. She had mine showing me how shallow David was."

Becky watched Cindy trying to read her face. Her voice held a note of truth but... Surely Dara would have mentioned that to Mel or even to her. What other secret dealings did Dara and Cindy have?

Melanie's hands dropped from her waist, and she stepped closer to Cindy, pleading with her eyes. "Okay. Say I believe you. After all that, you still want to leave? What about Dara? She asked the three of us to be here this weekend." She held her hands out. "Please stay. I promise, we'll never leave each other's side. We can do this."

Cindy shook her head. "Sorry. I've done enough for Dara. This is too much." She turned to Becky. "Where are the car keys?"

Chapter TWENTY

BECKY GOT UP from the bed and strode out of the room. Damned Cindy! Fine. She wanted to leave so bad, she could have the stupid car keys. She'd be out on her ass as far as the inheritance went. Behind her, Melanie was pleading with Cindy to stay. Cindy didn't even bother gracing the poor woman with an answer, following on Becky's heels.

The room was exactly as she'd left it the night before. The sprig of jasmine had wilted but was still on the pillow next to the bunched-up blankets. She snatched the set of car keys from the dresser and spun, throwing them at Cindy's head.

Cindy's hand flipped out and snatched them from the air in front of her face. Her smile was smug. "Remember? I'm the one who grew up with older brothers. I'm pretty fast, Becky."

She brushed by Melanie as she left the room. Becky could hear the door across the hall slam shut. She watched Melanie slouch into the room and sit on the end of the bed.

"This is so awful. How are we going to help Dara without Cindy? And I can't believe she's willing to walk away from that inheritance. I know she could use it." Melanie's fingers absently plucked at a piece of lint on her pajamas.

But Melanie's tone of voice was flat belying her words. She didn't sound all that broken up. Was it possible that she was happy that Cindy was leaving, that there'd be more of an inheritance split between just the two of them now? Melanie had downplayed the money element but had that been genuine?

Becky wandered over to the bed and placed her hand on Mel's shoulder. "It looks like it's just us now. We really need to stick together. No secrets; no wandering at night. This is important, Mel." She'd tie their hands together if she had to, to keep an eye on Melanie. Especially that night, when she'd planned some kind of séance. Perhaps with Cindy leaving that was off the table. Hopefully.

101

At the sound of Cindy's footsteps, Becky looked over at the doorway. She'd changed once more into her high heels and splashy clothes. No time for makeup, but she still looked attractive with the reddish curls falling over her shoulders. Again, the similarity between Cindy and Dara struck her anew. Except for the hair color and Dara's darker complexion they could have been twins.

"Well? Change your mind? It's not too late you know. There may be strength in numbers if we all leave. That lawyer set us up, and we'd have a good case to contest that provision in the will." She stood there dangling the keys, her other hand on the handle of her suitcase.

For a few beats Becky considered Cindy's point about contesting the will. There was no way she wanted to stay in the creepy, old resort with just Melanie. But Cindy could be wrong. And she'd be leaving that money not to mention anything about letting Dara down on the last request she'd ever make of them.

Becky shook her head and squeezed Mel's shoulder. "No. We're staying. Do us a favor, though, will you? Contact that lawyer, and let Hank know I'm fine. A police visit to check the place for intruders wouldn't hurt either."

"No problem. But for the record, I think you two are crazy. Your lives are at risk staying here. Dara died here. You idiots might be next." Cindy held her head high and then turned, her feet clacking on the wooden floors.

Melanie stood up. "Let's get something to eat. Then we can have a shower and get dressed. We don't need Cindy. We can do this. We were always closer to Dara than she was, despite her far-fetched tale of Ponzi schemes."

She was trying to be upbeat so Becky decided to join in. "So, tell me about this hot fireman. Now that Cindy's gone, I'd like to know more." She didn't really, but they had to pass the time. And what better way to crowd out the eerie events than with Melanie's sexual adventures. Dull though they might be.

Melanie's eyes brightened and she grasped Becky's arm. "You have to promise to keep this between us. It's kind of unconventional, y'know."

Becky's head tilted; this might be worthwhile after all. They entered the reception room, and her jaw tightened seeing that Cindy had left the door wide open. So like Cindy, totally self-centered. As long as she was safe, nothing else mattered.

"Hang on, Mel. Let me shut the door and then I'm dying to hear the down and dirty details."

She looked down the driveway and her eyebrows rose high seeing the car still parked there. The driver's door flew open and Cindy jumped out. With two hands she slammed the door as hard as she could, the car rocking from the impact.

At Melanie's warm breath on the back of her neck, Becky jumped. Melanie really was like a cat. She even had a catlike grin, her eyes soft slits. "I guess she had car problems, huh?" She turned, and as she walked back to the kitchen, she hummed a tune.

Becky turned and looked at Melanie just before she disappeared through the door entering the kitchen. She hadn't seemed in the least surprised to see the car still there. Even before Cindy stomped up the front steps, cursing about the car which wouldn't start, Becky knew that Melanie had something to do with it.

"The battery is dead as a doornail." Cindy had dragged the oversized suitcase to the table, and she plopped down in the chair next to it.

Becky walked over slowly. "So, you're stuck here with us whether you like it or not." She couldn't stop the smile that twitched on her lips.

"Screw that. Once I change my shoes I'm walking back to that town. It can't be farther than ten or fifteen miles. I'll be there in a few hours." She toed the high heels off and unzipped the suitcase. As she slipped her Nikes on, she looked up at Becky. "You should come with me. We both know that Melanie did something to the car last night.

She had it all planned out right down to recording the sound of her snoring. She's batshit crazy. Neither one of us need the money that badly to risk our lives."

Becky's stomach tightened listening to Cindy. Finally, she blurted, "I agree with you about the car. That was not only stupid of her, it puts all of us at risk, not being able to get out of here. She's not the same Melanie we knew in college."

Cindy looked up at Becky. "Did we ever really know her? C'mon. You know I'm right. Think about it. Come with me."

Becky could feel her shoulder slump in resignation. "I can't. I can't just leave her here on her own. You know she won't leave. She needs me, and if I desert her now and something happens...well, I couldn't live with myself."

Cindy shook her head as she stood up. "Suit yourself."

"I don't think you should go either. Look, it's only one night. If we stick together, we can get through it. That's what Dara asked of us in the will. This other stuff, 'saving' her soul is something Melanie cooked up. We don't have to do anything except be here until four tomorrow afternoon."

"Bullshit. You're trying to come off as the great arbitrator like you were when we all roomed together. But I'm not buying it. It's the money. Be honest with yourself at least." Cindy checked her waistband for the gun and then took a deep breath. "I will contact the lawyer and Hank when I get to town. Good luck. You're going to need it in this hellhole."

Becky watched her walk across the room and out the door. Now it was just her and Melanie left to face whatever. She took a deep breath and went into the kitchen.

Melanie stood at the stove, stirring a pan full of scrambled eggs. She looked over at Becky, and her eyebrows formed question marks. "Where's Cindy?"

"She's walking to town. Why'd you sabotage the car, Mel? That was stupid. What if one of us got hurt and needed to get out of here in a hurry? Now we're totally cut off." Becky folded her arms across her chest while her gaze skewered Mel.

Melanie's hand shot up like a traffic cop. "Now wait a damn minute!" She turned the heat down and faced Becky. "You think *I* did something to that car?"

"Hell, yeah! You don't seem all that surprised it didn't work!"

"Look Becks, I didn't do *anything* to that car. Although, frankly, I'm not surprised that it didn't start. This is not a nice place." She scanned their surroundings. "They're punishing and playing with us." She sighed. "I wish you'd believe me."

Becky folded her arms across her chest. "Oh. Just like that, I'm supposed to believe you?"

"I said I wasn't surprised. Listen—I don't know a damn thing about cars, okay? I don't even have a driver's license!" When Becky's eyes blinked in surprise, she added, "Honest, Becky! I don't!" Her eyes got a little wild. "How can I make you believe—" She stopped herself. She turned from the stove, stepping into Becky's space. Slowly drawing an 'X' over her chest, she said, "Cross my heart, Becky. On Dara's soul, I swear I didn't do anything to that car."

"On Dara's soul?"

"Yes!"

A cold dread rose in Becky's gut. She'd desperately wanted to find some reasonable explanation. What if Melanie hadn't sabotaged the car? That would leave...

She shook her head and took a deep breath. She couldn't go down that path. With Cindy gone, it was even more important to be logical and strong. She went over to the bank of drawers that had all slammed open on their own the night before. She pulled the top one out and peered into the empty space, trying to find some mechanism that might have caused it to fly out. But all she saw was the dark wood at the back of the cabinet, no lever or mechanical device. Her hand felt the drawer back, but again, nothing unusual.

"Can you wash some forks and knives, Becky? These eggs are done. We need to eat." Melanie proceeded to grab a couple of plates and dish out two servings.

She was still gripped with unease as she rinsed the cutlery. She glanced at the chair that she'd seen suspended against the wall. There was no reasonable explanation for that either. And she couldn't blame Melanie for that happening—not that time. Maybe Mel was telling the truth about the car. That was a grim thought.

"Grab the toast from the toaster and bring it in with the cutlery." Melanie called over her shoulder as she pushed the door to the reception room wide.

Becky dried the cutlery and grabbed the toast, hurrying after Mel. She had no wish to be alone in the kitchen any longer than necessary.

Melanie placed the plates on the table and then sat down waiting for Becky. From the expression on her face, she was still miffed about the car accusation. She plucked the cutlery up and silently began eating.

Becky suppressed a sigh of frustration. Melanie should be grateful that she hadn't left like Cindy wanted her to. "Look Mel, let's just try to get along. That's what Dara would have wanted, right?"

For a moment, Melanie was silent, staring at her plate. When she looked up at Becky, her eyes welled with tears. "She also wanted me to go to the lake last night. After we shower and dress for the day, I'd like to go down there again." She reached for Becky's hand. "You'll come with me, won't you?"

Becky suppressed the sigh and forced lightness into her voice. "Of course. We stay together from now on, watching each other's back. That's the only way this is going to work, Mel." She watched Mel closely, wondering what she'd try next in this insane quest to contact Dara.

***

A half an hour later, showered and wearing fresh clothes, Becky stood at the mirror in her room. She tugged her damp locks into a loose ponytail, listening for any sound coming from next door to indicate that Melanie was also close to being finished. Setting the comb on the wooden surface, she was about to turn when movement in the mirror caught her eye.

She froze watching the mirror as a shadow passed across the room behind her. Terrified, she spun around, but the only thing visible now was the bed and the empty space between it and the wall. The hair on the back of her arms tingled, and she had a hard time controlling her breathing as she stood peering at the room. She could have sworn there'd been something there. And the window was far enough away that it couldn't have been a trick of the light.

Hurrying from the room, she saw Melanie step out into the hallway. "Mel! I saw something...some dark shape next to the bed."

Mel tilted her head. "What? You saw a ghost or something?"

"Yes! No! I don't know. It was dark and moved really fast. I caught it from the corner of my eye when I looked in the mirror. But when I turned, it was gone!"

Melanie's eyes grew wide, and her hand rose to the neckline of her T-shirt scooping some necklace or chain from inside. Her fingers closed around what looked like a dark stone. Melanie must have noticed her confusion because she volunteered, "It's a protective amulet." She rushed over, and her other hand closed on Becky's arm.

Melanie led the way into the room, her footsteps slow as she peered around. Behind her, Becky's body felt tight as a coiled spring, her gaze taking in everything at once. Christ! She'd been in the shower totally vulnerable while some creepy thing was lurking in the bedroom. It had been just a fleeting glance, but there was no doubt that it had been there.

"I don't see anything, but I don't like the feeling in this room. The air...it's thick or something. Do you feel it?" Melanie glanced back at Becky, her face scrunched like she was smelling something foul.

Becky shook her head. "I don't feel anything, but I know what I saw."

"I believe you." Melanie scooped the comb and face cream from the dresser and tossed them into the open suitcase. As she zipped it shut, she glanced at Becky. "You're staying in my room from now on. I don't like the vibes in this one. We were going to stay together anyway."

Becky helped her with the suitcase, her hands trembling as she grabbed the handle. Shit. They'd separated for all of ten minutes or so to shower. Now, even that short time apart wasn't safe.

"Come on." Melanie waited for her to dart ahead, racing out the door before she followed and closed it.

Becky pulled the suitcase into Melanie's room and set it near the chair at the window. She stood trying to get her breath evened out, clasping and rubbing her upper arms. She had to get a grip on herself. There was still one night to get through before she could put some distance between this hellhole and sanity. She stepped closer to the window and peered out, making a sweep of the area from the trees to the driveway where the disabled car was parked.

"It'll be okay, Becky." Melanie walked over and placed her arm around Becky's shoulders. "I can only imagine how scary that was for you. Especially since you never believed in any of this before."

"Well, I'm sure coming around now." She slowly shook her head in amazement. "I can't believe I just said that."

"Don't worry, it's really not as crazy as you think."

"Easy for you to say." For a second Becky's eyes went wild with fear. "What are we supposed to do? How can we handle being here? Even for one more night?"

Melanie gave her shoulders a squeeze. "I got this. I've read and researched." She slipped the stone out again so that it dangled between her breasts. "Hence the obsidian stone."

Becky wasn't sure how much good that would do when night fell. She watched as Melanie leaned forward, her nose almost touching the glass of the window.

"What the hell?" Melanie shot a quick look over at Becky and then smiled when she gazed out the window again. "I think Cindy changed her mind. Look!"

Becky snuggled in close to Melanie at the glass. Oh my God. Cindy was racing up the driveway! She'd been gone almost an hour since she set out. So why was she back again?

But Becky's shoulders loosened a bit seeing her. At least they'd all be together to face the night.

Chapter TWENTY-ONE

THIS TIME, BECKY TOOK THE LEAD, racing from the room and down the hallway to the reception area. The door burst open, and Cindy staggered in, gulping air. There was a reddish glow to her skin and she bent forward, hands on her knees.

"What's wrong? You look like you ran all the way back here." Becky strode over to Cindy, looking outside before shutting and locking the door. Cindy waved her away as she struggled to get enough wind to be able to speak.

"I'll get her some water." Melanie raced across the room to the kitchen.

"I saw them." Cindy straightened and then trudged over to the chair and fell into it. She looked up at Becky and swallowed hard. "There was a car parked when I came to a bend in the road. Two guys were there talking—one old guy and a young guy in his twenties. They didn't see me."

Becky's eyes narrowed, and she pulled up a chair next to Cindy. The cold reality of what Cindy was getting at began to sink in. "The intruders. The guys that lawyer hired to scare us, right?"

Melanie came back into the room and handed the bottle of water to Cindy. "What happened that you had to run all the way back here?"

Becky answered for her, seeing that Cindy was downing almost the whole bottle of water. "She saw the guys who've been trying to scare us—the ones that lawyer hired."

Melanie shook her head. "Becky. You know what you saw earlier in your room. The things that have happened here weren't caused by anyone she saw. I don't know who she saw, but they've got nothing to do with what's going on here. They could have been hunters or *hikers* even."

Cindy banged the bottle of water onto the table. "It's them! Don't you see? They parked the car just far enough away that we'd never see it.

Then they walked here. They've been playing tricks on us since we got here. From the flowers to rigging the kitchen."

Melanie's argument aside—which Becky couldn't refute anymore—there was something that didn't add up. "But you never confronted them? It's not like you weren't armed. You should have asked them what the hell they were doing out here?"

"No. Don't you see? If that lawyer put them up to this, we have to stick it out. Sure, there's the money, but also, I'm not going to be manipulated like that. He can go to hell! He doesn't know who he's screwing around with." Cindy smiled, obviously enjoying the prospect of making a fool out of the lawyer.

Melanie's head tipped looking over at Becky. "Well? Do you tell her or do I?"

Becky's chin lowered as she leaned closer to Cindy, squeezing her hand. "That isn't all of it, Cindy. Even if they were here yesterday setting out the flowers and banging around to scare us, there's been too many things that they *couldn't* have caused—that chair suspended, the drawers and the wineglass with Dara's lipstick. You're grasping at straws. Trust me, I'd rather believe it was them than what's really going on in this place."

Cindy sighed. "You're sounding just like Mel, Becky. All I'm saying is it's possible, okay? Just because we don't know how they did it, doesn't mean they didn't. I admit I was scared earlier. I bolted out of here like a frightened rabbit, but when I saw them, standing there talking and then setting off into the woods, it just seemed like the most plausible explanation."

Melanie's eyes were flinty when she looked at Cindy. "And of course, the money didn't even cross your mind, huh? You were even willing to second-guess what you yourself encountered to get your hands on that money. You're a liar and a hypocrite, Cindy." She walked over to the door and opened it. "I'm going down to the lake. There's something there that I'm supposed to see. Are you two coming?"

Becky didn't hesitate in following Melanie. She'd hit on the real reason Cindy had returned. It had nothing to do with Dara or even any sense of loyalty to her friends. It was the money, pure and simple.

"What's she trying to do now? More stuff to scare us?" Cindy's chair banged over backward when she stood up. "I'm coming with you. I don't trust you any more than you trust me. Either of you."

Becky ignored Cindy as she walked down the steps. Melanie was just up ahead, striding fast to get to the lake which was a good hundred yards away. In the distance the mountain range was a hulking backdrop, the misty tops fading into the overcast sky. Tall grass and weeds clutched at her jeans as she strode over what once might have been a pretty garden area. Dampness clung to every blade of grass, and it was slippery in spots where the ground dipped lower.

Melanie perched on a dock that was tilted and sinking into the water. She peered down into the lake while Becky carefully picked her way up to stand beside her. Like the sky, the lake was gray and murky from the storm the night before.

"This is the spot where she went in." Melanie turned her head and Becky saw tears filling her eyes. "I'm probably standing on the exact place where Dara stood that night. I can feel her presence. It's very strong here."

The dock shifted, sinking lower when Cindy stepped onto it to join them. She bent at the waist, looking hard into the depths of the water, "What's that? There's something down there."

Becky stared hard into the water but all she could see were a few weeds swaying a few inches below the surface. "What? What am I supposed to be looking for?"

Cindy crouched down until she was kneeling on the old wooden planks, reaching into the water. "There's something lighter down there. Beside the middle weed...something lighter and shiny. A necklace?"

"Let me! I'll get it." Melanie pushed by Becky almost knocking her into the water.

She barely kept her balance watching Cindy grin and then slip off the dock, landing in water up to her shoulders. All the while, Melanie, laying flat on the dock reached into the water close to where Cindy was. "I see it!"

But Cindy sunk lower, disappearing under the surface. When she rose, shaking her head to clear the hair that had fallen over her face, she grinned. Trailing through her fingers were the fine strands of a gold necklace and a heart-shaped locket. When Melanie's hand rose to swipe it from her, Cindy jerked back.

"Oh, no you don't, Mel. I remember this locket. Dara's father gave it to her when she graduated." Cindy's fingers worked at the heart-shaped object trying to open it.

Becky stepped closer to the edge trying to see what Cindy saw. It did look familiar. It had to be Dara's.

"Give it to me!" Melanie's voice was like she'd regressed to being a six-year-old, all high-pitched and whiny. "I was the one meant to find this! She wanted me to come to the lake, remember?"

"Wow." Cindy looked over at them with wide eyes. She held the locket higher, still out of Melanie's reach and showed them what was inside.

There was a picture of an older man but his eyes were missing, like someone had taken a knife and scratched the photo obliterating them. Becky's chest hitched a breath as she peered at it. It had to be Dara who'd done that, mutilating the photo of her father. But why in the world would she?

"She threw that away just before she went off this dock. It was probably her final act of defiance to him before she drowned." Melanie pushed herself higher so that she was now squatting on her haunches.

Cindy waded closer to the dock and then handed Melanie the locket. "Here. I don't want this thing. It just seems so wrong to do that to his photo even if she hated him. He was her father after all."

Melanie snatched the locket from Cindy. "This is a message; don't you see? We were meant to find this." She rose higher and looked at Becky. "We'll need this for the séance. It's the last thing she touched."

"Séance?" Cindy hauled herself back onto the dock. She looked up at Becky and Mel. "Things aren't creepy enough here, that you two are seriously going to do a séance? On Dara's birthday?" She shook her head slowly. "Now that's really creepy."

"It's the best chance we have of contacting her," Melanie said, her voice firm. "Tonight her birthday coincides with the Autumn Equinox. Powers will be in the strongest alignment."

"Now you're getting weird." Cindy turned to Becky. "And you're all good with this crazy stuff?"

Becky nodded. "Apparently so." She shuddered thinking of the night ahead. But Melanie had been right about following Dara's guidance in coming to the lake. It was as if everything had been planned in advance and tonight would be the culmination.

Chapter TWENTY-TWO

WITH THE LOCKET FIRMLY IN HAND, Melanie stepped off the dock and started back up the slope to the resort.

"Hey! You're welcome!" Cindy jeered, scowling at Melanie's back. She looked up at Becky and extended her hand. "Help me up, will ya?"

Becky took her hand and pulled. "You need to get out of those wet clothes before you catch a cold."

"What I need is a hot shower and then something to eat. You guys had breakfast, but I left before then, remember? I'm starving." Cindy grumbled, falling into step beside Becky.

"Use Melanie's shower. That's the new plan. We stick together and stay in her room." She cast a look over at Cindy and pressed on. "I saw something in my room earlier—some shadow thing. That's why I know that those guys you saw have nothing to do with what's going on here."

Cindy shook her head, gaping at her. "How much sleep did you get last night? You don't think that maybe being tired and scared may have something to do with jumping at shadows? The place is strange, I'll give you that. But don't discount the men I saw earlier. It's an awful lot of money. This could be rigged out like a carnival house of horrors for all we know."

Becky examined Cindy's face, wanting desperately to believe her, yet her gut instinct was screaming otherwise. She knew in a week's time she'd look back and think it was silly to be worried about spirits and hauntings. Even so, right here and now she'd hedge her bets. There was some weird shit going on; it would be best to keep an open mind and be vigilant.

They'd reached the front steps where Melanie waited. Becky flashed a look at Mel. "We'll stay in your room while Cindy showers and changes her clothes. After that, I'll make lunch while you two keep me company. We stick together like glue until this weekend is over."

"Of course." Melanie's face softened when she looked at Cindy who was soaked to the skin and shivering. "Thanks for giving me the locket. Even if it was mainly the money that motivated you to come back, for what it's worth I'm glad you're here. It's what Dara wanted—the three of us together."

Cindy sighed. "I know. And even though you two don't believe me, I felt like a louse deserting you. Now, can we go in so I can get changed and fed?"

Becky smiled. It was a reprieve from the fighting at least for a little while. She noticed the holster of the gun resting above the waistband of Cindy's yoga pants. "Hey, you forgot the gun when you went in the lake. Will it even work now?"

Cindy slid the gun from her pants and then stepped by Becky, holding it up and aiming it at the dock. Becky jerked back at the sudden deafening noise. An explosion of splinters burst from one of the planks of the dock. Even though her ears rang she tapped Cindy's shoulder. "Point taken." She could hardly hear her own voice from the thrum against her eardrums.

Melanie's eyes were wide watching Cindy lower the gun. "If those guys are anywhere near, that should scare them away. Shit, it scared the hell out of me!"

"Yeah, at least they now know we're armed. I dare them to come within a mile of this place." Cindy walked past Becky and Mel and opened the door. She stepped inside and then strode over to grab her suitcase.

Becky followed Cindy when she crossed the floor and opened the door to where their rooms were. Her hand rose to rub at neck muscles which had tightened into a vice-like grip. Seeing Cindy firing the gun so naturally should have given her extra assurance that Cindy could handle it if necessary.

But the exact opposite was occurring. What if Cindy used that weapon on her and Melanie? She knew the statistics, even for accidental shootings. And with thirty million dollars on the line...well that could tempt even the most decent person.

When they entered Melanie's room, Cindy put the gun on the dresser and then rummaged around in her suitcase for clean, dry clothes. Becky glanced over at Melanie and saw that she was eyeing the weapon. There was a deep furrow in Melanie's brow, and her lips were a tight straight line.

"Okay. Give me ten minutes and I'll be with you. You don't mind if I use your shampoo do you, Mel?" Cindy grasped the bundle of clothes, walking over to the bathroom.

"No. Help yourself." Melanie's voice was soft and distracted.

When the door snicked closed behind Cindy, Becky stepped over to Melanie. "I don't like having that gun around. Hearing it go off, and seeing how it ripped into the dock really made it real for me—how *dangerous* it is. We both know what we're facing here. That gun's not going to stop it, and it just might get us killed."

Melanie nodded quickly. "My thoughts too. We've got to hide it from her."

Becky picked up the gun and then stepped over to the bed. Grabbing the corner of the mattress, she lifted it high enough to shove the gun as far as it would go on the box spring. She let the mattress fall again and then straightened the covers. "There." She looked over at Mel. "We both know where it is in the unlikely event we'll need it."

She straightened and listened to the hiss of the shower coming from the bathroom. "She's really going to be pissed with us, but I don't care."

"She'll get over it. It's not like we won't give it to her tomorrow. This just evens the playing field." Melanie flipped the locket open and peered at the ruined photo.

Becky stepped over, looking at it as well. A shiver rippled through her shoulders and she rubbed her upper arms. The photo of Dara's father made her skin crawl. Dara had obliterated his eyes and then cast the piece of jewelry away probably minutes before she drowned. "It's as if he killed her, isn't it?"

A blood-curdling scream pierced the air! Immediately after, a thud shook the floor.

Becky spun around watching the bathroom door where it had come from. Melanie leapt by her flinging the door wide. "Cindy?"

A cloud of steam poured from the room, revealing Cindy laid out on the floor. Melanie raced to her side. "Cindy! Oh my God! She's not moving!"

Becky wasn't even aware of how she got there, her heart thundering in her chest as she squatted down next to their friend. Her fingers flew to Cindy's neck checking for a pulse. There was a streak of blood at her hairline, and her eyes were closed. "Oh my God!" She breathed a sigh of relief feeling the steady beat under her fingertips. "She's unconscious, but she's alive!"

Melanie's head fell forward. "Thank you, Jesus!"

"She must have slipped in the bathtub and hit her head." Becky reached for the towel hanging on the bar and covered Cindy's body. She stood up and leaned in to shut the shower off.

"Cindy? Come on, honey, wake up." Melanie smoothed her hair back and leaned in to examine the cut on Cindy's forehead. She looked over at Becky. "What should we do? What if she doesn't wake up?"

"She will. We should get her to the hospital, but that's not going to happen with no car, is it? And no cell phones either. Great. Bunch up a towel and put it under her head, We should also turn her to the side in case she throws up." Becky helped Melanie with lifting Cindy's head and placing the towel there.

Suddenly Cindy's head shook and immediately after her feet flailed out, kicking. "What? What are you doing? Why am I on the floor?" Her eyes were wide but focused glaring at Becky and Mel.

"Easy. Just be still, Cindy. You fell and hit your head." But the fact that Cindy was agitated and responding with fear was actually a good thing. Becky smiled and swiped a tear from her eye. Thank God she hadn't hit her head harder.

"You scared the hell out of us, Cindy." Melanie grabbed the cloth from under Cindy's head and dabbed at the line of blood on her forehead.

"Wait!" Cindy clutched the towel to her chest and slowly came to a sitting position. "I remember! I didn't slip and fall. Someone shoved me! I grabbed at the shower curtain but... Oh my God. It was so strong. I *flew* through the air."

Becky's stomach grew tight with dread. *Pushed*? She looked over at Melanie and saw her own feelings echoed in the wide-eyed look on the other woman's face. Something had actually attacked Cindy. Hard enough that she could have been seriously injured.

Cindy looked from Becky to Melanie and back again, her eyes growing wider. "Oh my God. I wish it had been one of you that pushed me but it wasn't." She looked over at the bath tub and her jaw snapped shut.

Becky's heart hammered against her rib cage. It was hard to breathe. In a low voice she said, "Maybe...maybe we *should* get out of here."

But Cindy shook her head slowly from side to side. "I'm not leaving. This just got real personal for me." She looked over at the shower. "Hear that? Fuck you and the horse you rode in on! I ain't leaving!"

Chapter TWENTY-THREE

BECKY'S HEAD FELL BACK and she sighed. She knew all too well what that look on Cindy's face meant. She was totally pissed and out for revenge. There was no way she'd ever be able to convince either of her friends to leave. Yet, with every minute they stayed, the danger increased.

Melanie got to her feet and looked down at Cindy. "You've got a nasty cut on your forehead. I'll try to find a Band-Aid and some antiseptic ointment for it."

"Thanks." Still clutching the towel close, Cindy started to push herself up from the floor. Becky helped her to her feet while Melanie headed out.

"Oh shit..." Mel had frozen in place staring at the mirrored medicine cabinet. Her voice quivered. "Oh my God. There's a message on the glass. 'Help me. The altar. You have to...' But the next words are smeared."

Becky and Cindy crowded in behind Mel. A lot of the steam had cleared from the room but the mirror was still fogged up. There in the center of the glass, clearly written in large letters that drooled with condensation was the message. Becky's eyes almost popped out onto her cheekbones and she barely dared to breathe.

Cindy's voice was shrill, causing both Becky and Mel to jump. "What the hell? What does that even mean? What altar? What do we have to do?"

Melanie turned, and the whites of her eyes rimmed blue irises. "Dara wrote this, don't you see? She's sending a message to us."

Cindy's teeth ground so hard they crunched. "It better not have been Dara shoving me out of that shower! So help me."

Melanie shook her head. "Dara would never hurt any of us. No. That was the others. The ones that want us to leave." She looked at Becky. "I know this scared you. Hell, it scares me! You wanted us to go,

120

but the attack had the opposite effect on Cindy. Dara knew that, and she left us this message."

Becky still wasn't convinced that leaving should be off the table, even if Mel was right that it had been Dara leaving the message. "Cindy probably should see a doctor, Mel. Head injuries aren't something to take lightly. We should go."

Cindy waved her hand dismissing Becky's comment. "I'm fine. Think that's the first time I was knocked unconscious? Older brothers, remember?" She stared at Melanie. "Wait a minute. You said that Dara wanted you to go to the lake, that there was something she wanted you to see there. Now she's letting us know there's some altar on the property? First the locket and now this. But what does she want us do if we find it? How can we help her?"

For a few moments they were silent, thinking, but then Becky spoke. "Find the altar. We've been upstairs in this wing, and there's nothing up there, no sign of an altar. The other two wings look pretty rough as well. Hell, the whole place is a wreck. And why would there be an altar at a resort? Do Jewish people even *have* altars? I've never been in a synagogue."

Melanie looked off to the side, silent for a few beats. "Wait. There's another possibility. Altars are used in religious ceremonies but they're also used in satanic ones."

"Satanic? Like in witchcraft or something?" Becky was still trying to come to terms with why an altar would be at a resort let alone bringing in some dark magic element. She looked at the message again in case they'd got it wrong, but no it clearly spelled "'altar.'"

"Hang on!" Cindy stared hard at Melanie. "What if it's not Dara leaving the message? Don't forget something pushed me out of the shower. Maybe the message is from whatever did that!"

But that couldn't be true. Even though all of this supernatural stuff was a stretch for Becky, she had to disagree. "This message asks for our help. The bad things that Melanie insists are here and who have been doing everything to get us to leave, even attacking Cindy; they want us to leave, not help them. I'm with Mel on this; it had to be Dara who left the message."

Even though Melanie nodded in agreement, Becky pushed on. "Was Dara involved with some cult? Would she have been part of this Satanic thing you mentioned? That's assuming that it *is* some sort of black magic or hoodoo thing, which I'm not convinced of."

"No way! Dara became interested in the supernatural after her father died. She came to visit me to enlist my help in contacting him. I know Dara. She would have told me if there was anything more to what she was doing—that she'd become involved with some cult or witchcraft."

Cindy patted herself dry with the towel and reached for her clothes, turning away from them. "Okay. She wanted to contact her father but then she mutilates his photo suggesting that she became very angry with him. Angry enough that she threw the locket away."

Melanie's mouth fell open and she grasped Becky's arm. "When we commented on that...that's when Cindy got pushed from the shower."

Becky looked past Cindy staring around the room for any other sign of the dark entities. "That thing I saw in my room earlier. That was one of these things, wasn't it? But the message was from Dara. If those bad spirits had something to do with Dara's death, they're still threatening her. She writes the message, and Cindy gets shoved so hard she just about gets a concussion."

Melanie nodded. "That's what I've been trying to tell you. Dara is here and she needs our help. She's trapped, held prisoner somehow. And somehow, she had premonitions that this would happen. That's why she wrote the letter to us."

Cindy turned to face them. "If it's all the same to you, can we get out of this place? I mean the bathroom. We can finish this conversation while I eat. This room seriously creeps me out." She zipped up the bright pink hoodie she'd slipped on.

Becky didn't need to be asked twice. She followed Cindy from the room but looked back before closing the door. Melanie was still gazing at the message in the mirror. "C'mon, Mel."

Heading back to the kitchen, Cindy resumed the conversation.

"Why did Dara buy this place? I mean aside from the obvious—to make money. Was there some kind of connection that her family had with it? I know that in its heyday this area was known as the Borsch Belt. In the fifties and sixties, many affluent Jewish people escaped the summer heat in big cities to vacation here. Dara's family was Jewish."

Melanie nodded. "There could be something there. She would have been too young but maybe her father or grandparents stayed here. I wish we had our phones and an internet connection to do some more digging on this." She looked over at Becky. "I think she found some kind of connection between her family and this place. A connection that involved something dark."

They left the bedroom and wandered down the hall. Cindy led the way, looking over her shoulder at them when she spoke. "She must have known. She may have found out the extent of that connection after she bought it. There had to be some family history. Maybe old photos of her grandparents here?"

Becky stepped through the doorway after Cindy. "That could be. After her father died, she would have gone through all his papers. Maybe when you tried to contact her deceased father, this connection was what she was trying to confirm." Even as the words left her mouth, she felt like she'd gone down the rabbit hole along with Mel and Cindy. But this whole resort, Dara buying it and then dying here *was* a descent into a black hole.

"That altar. She wants us to find it and then what? She didn't tell us where it is which suggests she never found it." Melanie sighed. "Instead, she drowned. Whatever dark spirits are here, they defeated Dara before she could..."

Just as Cindy was about to enter the reception area, she stopped. "My gun. I forgot it."

Becky squared her shoulders, "No more guns, Cindy. What we're dealing with won't be stopped with a gun. We put it somewhere safe. We didn't feel comfortable with it being here. You'll get it back tomorrow."

Melanie nodded. "You were outvoted on that one, Cindy. Sorry."

Cindy's hands rose, her fingers splayed like she was ready to throttle them on the spot. "That's bullshit! It's my gun and I need it. Don't forget those two guys I saw."

Melanie gave Cindy's shoulder a light tap. "If they show up and threaten us, you'll get your gun back, I promise. But you of all people should realize the threat isn't them. Christ Cindy! You were attacked in the shower by some evil entity! Some spirit thing!"

Cindy's eyes flared. "By some *ghost.*"

The two of them stared at each other in apprehensive wonder.

Their realization was interrupted by Mel's voice. She was all business when she said, "We've got to try to find this altar that Dara warned us about."

Cindy turned. "Where's the locket?"

Melanie pulled it from the pocket of her jeans. She flipped it open again and stood looking at it. "The more I look at this photo the more convinced I am that Dara's father was mixed up in something bad that happened here. She knew it too."

There was silence for a few seconds as they crossed the reception area. Finally Melanie put words to the thought that Becky dreaded.

"We need to take stock of the rest of the resort, you guys. I'm not talking about going into those two other wings that you sealed off. We need to search the property, the grounds, for this altar."

Chapter TWENTY-FOUR

BECKY SHUDDERED going into the kitchen, her gaze darting over to where the chair had been suspended that morning. But everything was as they'd left it. Thank God.

Rummaging around in the fridge, she took out cold cuts and mayonnaise. "Sandwich okay, Cindy?" There were a few bottles of wine on the lower shelf which looked appealing right about then. Especially after what had happened earlier. But she took a pass, grabbing the loaf of bread and butter.

"Sure." Cindy joined her at the fridge, grabbing the cold cuts and a jug of milk. "After I eat, we'll begin the search for this altar." She looked over at Melanie. "You really think it's something to do with devil worship or witchcraft?"

Melanie nodded. "It's the only thing I can think of. If it were a Christian altar, why would it be here? No. Satanic rituals or witchcraft is often practiced outdoors."

Cindy paused in the midst of slicing the sandwich she'd thrown together. "But you also said you want to do a séance. That's probably not a great idea if you think there's some kind of demonic influence here. Have you any experience other than that time with Dara, trying to contact her father?"

Melanie leaned against the counter watching Becky and Cindy. "Of course, I've done some. There're always spirits who linger in this earthly dimension. They're usually confused or afraid to continue on to the next level, but here, it's more than that. There's such a feeling of hostility..." Her eyes darted around the room. "And *rage*."

Becky continued making Cindy's lunch, but Melanie's words had shot an arrow of fear straight through her bowels. "Doing a séance here sounds dangerous. What if—"

"They attack us again?" Cindy slammed the glass of milk on the counter, spilling some. "My head still hurts from getting pushed out of the shower." She stared at Melanie, "I know you want to connect with Dara and believe it or not so do I, but..." She took a deep breath. "Are we biting off more than we can chew?"

"There's no other way, I'm afraid." Melanie shook her head slowly. "I know there's risks but we have to chance them. We need to find out more about what happened that night and how we can help Dara. I know she's trying to communicate as much as she can, but there're limits to what she can do. The séance will provide a clearer conduit for her."

Cindy held up a hand. "You mean for her to talk to us?"

"Kinda, yeah. To communicate with us directly, yes."

A shudder rippled through Becky's shoulders when she looked over at Melanie. "A clearer conduit for whatever else is here as well. These things led to Dara's death. We all agree on that. There's got to be another way without exposing ourselves to that degree of danger. Cindy could have been killed, and that's even before we invite these things in for a *chat*."

Cindy grabbed the sandwich and put it on a plate before leading the way into the reception area. "Come on. Let's look at everything we know so far and try to figure out a plan to protect ourselves. I don't want to do this séance either, but I agree with Mel. We have to help Dara."

Becky remembered what Mel had done the night before. "What about salt, Mel? You used that to keep the bad spirits away from us. We can try that."

Melanie sat at the head of the table while the other two took their usual seats. "Of course, we'll use that. But it may not be enough. That's why I want to explore the resort to find that altar. There's something old and evil here that wants us gone. And Dara's father has something to do with it."

Cindy swallowed the food in her mouth and leaned over the table, staring at them, "Following that logic, Dara's ancestors might have been devil worshippers. Who knows how the family came to be so wealthy? Isn't that a perk of going to the dark side?"

Becky sighed. If she wasn't so freaked out at the prospect of the night ahead, she'd dismiss what Cindy was implying out of hand. "You're actually speculating that someone in Dara's family sold his soul to the devil in exchange for riches." Oh my God. Was this conversation really happening? Tomorrow couldn't come fast enough.

"You got any better explanation? I'm all ears." Cindy rolled her eyes before continuing with her lunch.

"Hang on." Melanie's head dipped to the side, and she was quiet for a couple moments thinking. "There are Satanic cults all over the place. I don't exactly agree with Cindy, but I'm not ruling out blood sacrifice. Although from what I've read the sacrifice consists of small animals, not people."

Becky had heard enough. This was speculation. Now they were considering living sacrifices? "Come on! This was a resort for rich Jews, not Wiccan or witches or—"

"I didn't *say* witches! Satanic isn't witchcraft. We're skylarking here, Becky! There has to be a reason that this place is haunted with nasty spirits." Melanie sat back in her chair, defying Becky with her raised chin.

Becky felt like she'd stepped into the twilight zone. She snorted "Next, you're going to say the resort is built on ancient Indian burial grounds. There may be an altar, I get that, but *sacrifices*?"

Cindy finished eating and wiped her lips on the paper napkin that was next to her plate. "Well, there were pentagrams and stars drawn in the empty rooms that Becky and I saw. That kind of supports the Satanic theory."

"There were also 'Johnny hearts Sara' and totally out-of-proportion penises." Becky shook her head. "No. What we saw up there was the work of bored teenagers."

Melanie stood up. "Ready? Let's see what we can find out there."

"Wait a minute." Cindy grabbed her empty plate and dashed into the kitchen. When she returned there was a butcher knife in her hand. Seeing the look that Becky and Melanie shot her, she shrugged. "You won't let me have my gun so this will have to do. I'm not going exploring without something to protect us."

"Suit yourself." Becky followed Melanie out the front door and down the steps. Cindy was still worried about those two guys she saw. If only it were that simple. When she got to the bottom stair she turned to see what was keeping Cindy.

Cindy was squatted down wedging a stray leaf into the crack between the frame and the door. She rose and when she noticed the look of curiosity in Becky's eyes she scowled. "We don't have a key to lock it. If that leaf isn't there when we return, I'll know if those guys went in. We've got to cover all our bases."

Becky smiled. "I get it. Another trick you learned living with brothers."

"More like my mother sneaking into my room and poking around in my stuff. She was always freaked out about any of us getting into drugs." Cindy stepped quickly to catch up with her.

Becky picked her way along a slippery cobblestone pathway that skirted the east wing of the resort, past the garage where she and Cindy had found the nails. The air was heavy with humidity from the storm and the overgrown grass soaked through her sneakers.

"Look at that!" Melanie darted ahead.

Becky hurried after her and came to a stop. A swimming pool bordered by a chain link fence, was a broken concrete pit in the ground. Grape vines clung to the fence's metal posts that still stood, while small saplings managed to strive upward through the wide cracks in the concrete. The smell of rot and stagnant water drifted into her nostrils. "Yuck. Hard to believe this was once a pool."

Cindy stepped by her and came to a stop next to a broken and twisted metal lawn chair. "It's actually kind of sad. People lounged around this pool, watching their kids play in the water. They probably looked forward to their family vacation here, getting away from the rat race of the city."

"Memories." Melanie plucked a leaf from one of the small trees gazing down into the pool. "They were creating fleeting moments in time. It just goes to show you how fragile and temporary humans are compared to the force of nature."

Becky stepped over a heap of vines leaving the pool behind her. "Let's keep going." She saw the small patio off the kitchen entry about fifty feet away. The path leading to the forest at the back of it had caught her eye earlier. If there was anything dark and evil on the grounds, it was probably in that stand of trees. The hair on her arms spiked high watching the towering pines and oaks, their limbs arching over the path making it look like a dark tunnel.

"Wait. If we're going into those woods, I'd better take the lead." Cindy held the knife to the side, and a spark of light glinted off the sharp blade when she waved it.

A chill skittered through Becky's shoulders as she watched Cindy head to the dark wooded area. When she followed, she hugged her arms to her chest feeling the temperature fall and the light grow fainter. The air was deadly still and not a sound other than her breathing and the whisper of their sneakers on the flagstone could be heard.

Cindy looked back at them. "Shouldn't there be birds or even bugs flying around, making some noise?"

"It's like we've slipped into a kind of dead zone." Melanie's hands cupped her upper arms and she rubbed them briskly as she peered into the forest above and beside them. "I don't get a good feeling about this place."

Becky felt it as well. Her skin prickled with goose bumps and she slowed her pace, watching everything around her. And it wasn't just the stillness getting to her. There was a feeling that they were trespassing here and a greater feeling that their intrusion was not going unnoticed.

They rounded a bend in the path, and the flagstone ended abruptly, replaced now with a narrow walkway, slick with mud. Ferns and vines crowding the edge of the path obliterated it in some lower spots.

"Do you think we should keep going? I think it's just going to lead us back to the lake." Cindy's knuckles were ivory gripping the handle of the knife. Her face was tight and forehead furrowed.

"We have to. I know this place is creepy, but that's exactly why we need to keep going. If there's some kind of altar on the property, I'm betting it's in this forest." Melanie gnawed at her thumbnail, something she'd done in college the night before an exam.

Becky knew that like it or not, they weren't leaving without checking this part of the property out. A bead of cold sweat trickled down her spine but she nodded. "Don't get too far ahead of us, Cindy. We'll take it nice and slow." What was surprising even to her own ears was the fact that her voice had dropped to a whisper.

"You don't have to worry about that." Cindy took a step threading her feet through the underbrush, holding the knife out at her side. She slipped, barely managing to stay upright, her other hand grasping at the foliage nearby. "Shit! Careful. With that rain last night, this path is like a skating rink."

When Becky stepped forward, she felt her foot sink lower in the soil, the water seeping halfway up the sneaker. The bottom half of her jeans were completely saturated, clinging wetly to her shins. Every step was slow and slippery, wading through muck.

"Can you feel it?" Melanie was just behind her, hissing a whisper.

"I can barely feel my toes from all this water and cold mud." Becky glanced ahead, hoping for some break in the trees. The lake—anything. But all she saw was more of the same, dark spruce and cedar blotting out the pale gray sky.

"No. I mean the atmosphere. This is even stronger than in the house. Whatever is in here hates the fact that we're venturing into its lair."

Becky was about to turn to say something but spun around at Cindy's high-pitched yelp, just in time to see her crashing to the ground. She sat on the ground with a dazed look.

When they squatted down by her, she barked, "Shit! It happened again! Someone knocked my feet out from under me!"

"Or something," Melanie added as she helped Cindy to her feet. "Oh!" She pulled her hand from Cindy's forearm, her palm slick with blood. "You cut yourself! That knife. I knew you shouldn't have brought it."

Becky reached for Cindy's arm, examining the cut. It was about two inches long but not deep, thank God. She no longer had the knife in her hand.

"I'll live. It's just a scratch. Where'd the knife get to?" Cindy started to push at the undergrowth, swiping it away to find her weapon.

"Hang on. I see it!" Melanie stepped off the path, kicking through the small saplings and forest growth to get to it. She paused at a white birch and then bent over to get it. When she straightened, she peered through the gaps in the trees. "What the heck?" She swept through the brush and took a step deeper into the forest.

"What is it?" Becky's mouth was suddenly dry, and her heart had kicked up into overdrive. But Melanie ignored her, now walking faster through the trees.

"Mel! Come back. Or at least wait for us!" Cindy traipsed after Mel, leaving Becky behind.

Oh shit. There was nothing else except to follow the two of them. Becky winced at the brambles clawing her jeans when she stepped off the slick path. A glance through the trees showed Melanie's red sweater before she disappeared behind some mammoth pine. "Wait!" Even Cindy had dashed ahead, leaving her about twenty feet behind.

What the hell was wrong with them? They had agreed to stay together, and now they were all racing off, separating in these damn woods! A thorn on some bush pierced through the sleeve of her shirt and tore at her flesh. She pushed the sleeve higher and saw a line of red just below her elbow. Her teeth ground together at the sharp sting. Double shit!

She pushed ahead, holding her arms high and out of the way of any more brambles. Finally, she reached her friends. Her mouth fell open seeing what lay just ahead. Unlike the thicket of trees, they'd just scrambled through, she stood at the edge of a clearing. It was circular and about thirty feet across. Slate-gray flagstones covered the area. Her breathing quickened when she realized there was absolutely no overgrowth between the stones; it was as clean as if it had just been laid. She felt her heart pound in her chest when she saw the raised stone platform at the opposite end. On top of the platform was a single slab of stone, about five feet long and three feet high.

Melanie's voice was steady. "It's the altar. This is what we were looking for."

The three of them stood at the edge of the clearing in stunned silence. Finally, Melanie began walking across the stones to it. Becky and Cindy shot each other a look and followed.

Melanie stepped onto the platform and walked around the altar, gazing at its surfaces. "There're letters carved into it," she said in a low voice.

Becky's gaze flitted around to the glade of trees. She half expected a posse of black-robed Satanists to come rushing out of the woods. But the trees and underbrush remained still. Her knees knocking, she stepped up onto the platform beside Mel. Holding her arms tight to her body she peered to see what Mel was looking so intently at. The letters, black with mold were set out in a clear line down the center of the altar top. She leaned closer and read aloud. "That's a 'T', an 'H'... 'D'... 'M'..." There were more letters but they were hard to make out in the shadowy light. She brushed the surface of some fallen twigs and leaves. "That's an 'S'." The last letter was even harder to make out. She traced the surface, her finger following the chiseled shape. "I think it's a 'Z'.

Melanie's eyes met hers and she whispered, "S. Z. Wasn't Dara's father's name Saul? Saul Zuckerman."

"But you said her father would have been a child when this resort was up and running." Cindy had stepped over to join them, staring hard at the stone.

Becky was no rock expert, but one thing she was sure of was this thing was really old and—bad. Every cell in her body screamed at her to run. Get far away from this thing. She wiped her finger on her jeans.

Melanie was giving the stone a wide berth now, circling it to come around to join Cindy and her. She huddled close to them and her voice was barely above a whisper. "It could be Dara's grandfather. Lots of sons are named after their fathers. I really think Dara's family was involved in this."

Cindy turned slowly, peering down at the stones under their feet and examining the outer circle. She stepped over to one stone and bent lower. "Oh my God. Look at this."

Becky found it hard to breathe let alone speak, but she managed to squeak out the question, "What? What are you looking at?" They'd found the altar, so what other horror had she found?

Cindy joined Melanie at the side of the altar facing the clearing, and her hand rose to cup her throat as she followed Mel's gaze looking down at the flagstones. "Oh shit," she whispered.

Becky came around and stood beside them.

"Oh shitty shit shit," she said.

From the altar's vantage point, they saw the stones of the clearing's shape.

It was a pentacle.

Each of the stones had scrolls and other carvings on them.

"What is that?" Cindy asked pointing at them. "Some kind of voodoo hieroglyphics?"

Becky felt a wave of dread wash over her.

Mel's voice was hard. "It could be Satanic symbols...or some other dark occult stuff."

"What do they say?" Becky's voice cracked.

"I don't know. I've always avoided *anything* to do with that part of the occult. I only know they have their own symbols and stuff."

This was proof that not everything about the resort had been happy family vacations. There was a darker element, an evil presence that had lay secret and hidden from prying eyes. It was only a fluke that they'd wandered off the path to find it.

She whispered, turning to Mel, "This is witchcraft, isn't it? That platform is the altar."

"Sorcery for sure. From the vibes in this place the altar could have been used for sacrifices."

Becky had heard enough. The place was dark, and the air was hard to breathe. Just standing there made her heart pump faster. For the third time she looked over her shoulder waiting for something to happen. "We've found what we were searching for. There's a connection to the occult that explains in part why the resort is so creepy. Can we get out of these woods now?"

Shaking her head 'no', Cindy said, "I vote we stay on the path to find out where it leads. Maybe we'll find something that will explain Dara's message in the mirror. We found the altar but now what? There's got to be more." Cindy wasted no time in backtracking across the flagstone circle to the heavy undergrowth of the forest.

Becky saw Melanie hadn't even noticed Cindy' hightailing it; she was completely engrossed examining the altar and the symbols carved in it. Becky grabbed her arm and dragged her along, huffing, "C'mon. Cindy's getting ahead of us and we need to stick together. Especially now."

Melanie nodded. "Okay."

When Becky scraped through the brush and undergrowth heading back to the path, she saw that it was even narrower: barely wide enough to get through.

Becky hustled down the trail trying to keep Cindy in sight. Cindy's pink shirt was just up ahead, but the woman's lower half was enveloped in the forest growth. "Wait up!" Cindy didn't even pause or look back, dammit!

The air was damp and cold on Becky's skin as she shoved through the overgrown path. She hurried, despite slipping a few times on the slick surface. Judging from the wide curve, it looked like they'd be coming out of the forest soon.

Startled by the sudden loud cawing overhead, she looked up at an ancient oak tree. A flock of crows, black birds lined the branches, screaming down at her with high-pitched cackles. Her heart leapt high in her throat. Hundreds of angry crows with beady, black eyes stared down at her.

As soon as she made eye contact with one of them, they all went silent. A shiver trembled up her spine. It was more than just curiosity in their glistening eyes; there was malice. She stood stock-still watching them as they sized her up.

'A murder of crows' popped into her head.

She fled down the greasy path, racing to escape the dark woods and the evil-looking birds as well as that altar and *place*.

The air became warmer and brighter, the growth of trees less dense when she rounded the bend. The lake was about fifty feet away, the decrepit dock farther down the shore. Cindy stood watching the water when Becky emerged from the woods.

She turned to Becky and then looked past her into the forest. "Where's Mel?"

Becky spun around. "She was right behind me, I swear. What the hell is she doing *now*? God, I hope she didn't go back to that place."

"You should have waited—at least to make sure she didn't fall or something." Cindy brushed by Becky rushing back down the path into the woods, yelling, "Melanie?"

"You're the one who took off running! We were trying to catch up to you!" Her hands rolled into fists and she huffed a fast sigh, but she couldn't just stand by and let something happen to Melanie. She stomped back onto the path. It would be just like Mel to think of something about that altar and pentagram and double back to check it out on her own, never considering how they'd promised to stick together.

Never a thought about how they'd worry. She could be such a self-centered bitch sometimes!

Again, she rounded the curve in the path and looked up to see if the crows were still there. But there were only the branches reaching out from the trunk. She had seen and heard them earlier though. Hadn't she?

Cindy's voice broke the stillness in the forest, again calling for Melanie. Great. Mel wasn't even answering which meant she may even have gone all the way back to the hotel. "Cindy? Wait for me, will you? It's bad enough that one of us is missing let alone getting completely separated."

Becky strode after her, hurrying—again!—seeing Cindy on the path ahead. Her head spun at the sound of a branch snapping as loud as a firecracker from deeper in the trees. She peered through the old growth looking for any sign of Melanie. There was just a glimpse of red between the trees before a loud crashing sound and scream pierced her ears.

"Mel!" Cindy took off through the trees, bounding through the dense undergrowth like a spooked deer. "Melanie! Are you okay?"

Becky followed the broken trail that Cindy left. From the sounds of Melanie's scream, she was hurt or in trouble. Why had she wandered off the path in the first place?

She caught up with them, finding Cindy helping Melanie to her feet. "What happened?" Her eyes darted around the forest, checking for any threats.

Melanie was pale, and the whites of her eyes showed when she gaped at them. Leaves and dirt clung to her shirt where she'd taken the fall. "I saw her." Melanie stumbled to the side, and she reached out to grab a branch before she fell down again.

Cindy reached for her arm and pulled her close. "Saw who?"

Melanie pushed away from them, staring over at the growth of trees where she'd been headed. "Dara! She was right here!" Melanie started to walk away, going deeper into the forest but Cindy yanked her back. Melanie was like a rag doll against Cindy's strength.

"You aren't going anywhere! Especially not off on your own in *this* place. What exactly did you see?" Cindy was brooking no argument, even giving Melanie a little shake to get her to focus.

"It was *her*! She was wearing a white jacket, her hair streaming out behind her as she ran through the woods. Let's find her!" Melanie tried to pull away, but this time Becky stepped up to help hold her back.

"You can't go after her, Mel." Becky took a deep breath, trying to control her voice and sound reasonable despite the fact her whole body trembled. "You said it yourself, Mel. There's something evil in these woods. Do you honestly think you saw Dara? It might have been a trick of the light. But even if you did see something what would have been accomplished if you'd raced after it?"

Cindy's mouth fell open and then she blurted, "We'd be separated. That was its plan. And for sure Dara wouldn't want that."

Melanie's gaze flickered between them, and her shoulders fell as the truth of Cindy's words sunk in. "No! Dara wants us to help her! She would never, ever hurt us!" Her eyes took on a wild expression as the penny dropped. "Oh God..." she panted. "That wasn't Dara!" She stared at the spot in the forest she had been trying to get to and backed away from it slowly. "This place is bad. And it almost succeeded in separating us." Without another word she turned and began walking back to the path.

Cindy looked over at Becky and shook her head. "Let's get the hell out of here before whatever she saw comes back."

Chapter TWENTY-FIVE

MIKE DROGAN ADJUSTED THE SIGHTS on the binoculars as he peered through the lenses. "What are they up to now?" He stood on a ridge high above the resort while his much younger partner rested on a boulder taking a healthy swig of water.

"Let me take a look." Adam Rafferty rose and took the binoculars that Mike extended. When he zeroed in on the back of the hotel, the women were walking along a path that led to dense forest. The hair on the back of his neck spiked high just looking at the trees. "I don't like the looks of this."

"What do you mean? And don't give me none of that hocus-pocus shit." Mike folded his beefy arms over his chest and snorted.

Adam let the binoculars slip lower, and he shook his head watching his friend. "That so-called hocus-pocus shit is why you asked me here. I could be spending the weekend with my girlfriend but instead I'm practically soaked to the skin, *enduring your company* I might add, while we keep an eye on these women."

Mike cleared his throat to hide the chuckle that threatened to rise. It had been a while since he'd seen Adam, and even though it was an odd assignment, it was good to see the kid. But he couldn't let Adam know that, of course. "It's only till tomorrow afternoon. Then Wilson will return and dole out their checks. We just need to keep an eye out to make sure they're safe until then."

Adam felt his stomach tighten when he looked through the field glasses again. "Safe? They're staying in one of the most sinister spots I've ever come across."

Mike snorted. "That's a hell of a statement, considering your...experiences." He glanced back to the resort. "Wilson told me he puked after meeting them there yesterday. That's why he called me." He shot a look at Adam. "And specifically asked for you to tag along."

"Tag along. Yeah, right." Adam glanced at his feet and back over to Mike. "Wilson—his family doing okay?"

Mike coughed. "You mean *families*..."

"Whatev."

"Yeah, all's well for him, domestically. That case worked out well, didn't it?" He folded his arms, leveling a steady gaze at Adam. "Well enough that he smoothed everything over for you with the cops, back in the day, right?"

"Well, I *was* innocent!"

"Adam, there was enough circumstantial stuff to have the cops and prosecutors give you a real going over. Wilson saved your ass."

Nodding, Adam said, "Yeah. Yeah, he did." With a shrug, he added, "Which is why he called us on this case."

"C'mon, Adam!" Mike let out a guffaw. "Who the hell else could he call?" He made a pantomime of being on the phone. "Hello? Magnum PI? I'm a lawyer, and I want you to investigate a case involving thirty million dollars and some kind of supernatural shit going on at an abandoned resort." He made a faux look of surprise. "Hello? Hello? Damn, he hung up!" He looked back to Adam. "Instead, he phones me, tells me the place is so weird he puked his guts out and to bring you along. Boom, here we are."

Adam pointed at the hotel grounds. "That place oozes malice, Mike. As strong as what I dealt with back at Saranac Lake."

Mike went still. "Shit. Are you saying that...that *thing* is back?"

Adam made a small wave of his hand. "Nah. We won't be seeing that son of a bitch anymore." He gestured again. "But just because you get rid of one bad guy doesn't mean crime stops, does it?" He looked over to Mike. "You know that, man. You spent thirty years as a cop." He turned back to the resort. "That place should be burned down and bulldozed, man. Definitely *not* reopened."

"What is it about mountains? First the Adirondacks and now the Catskills." Mike grabbed the knapsack he'd lugged up there and jerked his head to the side, signaling the resort. "Maybe we'd better get closer. If this place is as bad as you say, we might have to move in fast."

Adam handed the binoculars back and then grabbed his own bag. "What kind of a friend makes it a condition in her will that they have to spend two nights in a place like that? With friends like that, you don't need enemies."

"I don't know. The lawyer wasn't clear on that part. Maybe she's haunting the place and wants a final hurrah with them." Mike led the way down the mountain, walking slowly to avoid slipping in the damp soil.

"She drowned there. I'd say the chances of her hanging around are pretty good. But it's the forest and the resort itself that gives me the heebie-jeebies. Even from a distance I get a strong vibe."

Mike kept his head down watching his footing. "Vibe. Well, that tells me...nothin'. Could you be a little more specific? Is it a stoner's vibe? A jazz musician's vibe?"

"Rage, man."

"Damn. I was hoping for something more innocuous, Adam."

"Sorry, Mike, nothing simple. There's a murderous anger that hangs over that place like a cloud. Hell, from what you said you don't even need a sixth sense to pick up on that. The lawyer did and so did one of the women."

Mike's face was grim when he looked over his shoulder, peering at Adam. "That's why we're here, bucko. I know I tease you about this hocus-pocus shit, but I've seen enough of your talent to pay it some serious respect." He smiled to lighten the mood. "Even if it means I've got to put up with your smart-ass mouth."

"I'm the son you wish you'd had. Face it, Mike. You love me." Adam clapped Mike on the back and then stepped quickly by him. If the old guy slipped, at least he'd be there to break the fall.

"Love you like a *toothache*," Mike grumbled, but there was warmth in his voice that he couldn't hide.

"Yeah, yeah." Adam glanced back at him. "So, everything was quiet last night when you were here alone?" That would be hard to believe. He'd felt the evil as soon as he'd seen the place. Giving it a wide berth trekking up the mountain was the easy part of this assignment.

"I wouldn't say it was quiet—not with the thunder boomers and the rain coming down in sheets. I could see in through the window from where I'd taken shelter, at least until the storm knocked the power out. I was just about to call it a night when one of them, the blond, wispy one came out the door and wandered down to the lake. She was out there about ten minutes before she had the sense to go back inside."

Adam paused before stepping past a large boulder. "And again, today they went down to the lake. At least this time they found what they were looking for, even if one had to take a dip in the water to get it." He continued walking grabbing at branches of scrub cedar and bushes to keep from lurching forward.

Behind him, Mike stopped. "Let me catch my breath for a second, okay?" He shook his head. "Coming down this damn hill is tougher than I thought!" He jabbed a finger at the resort buildings before them. "Maybe we should have moved in when we heard that scream earlier."

Adam had turned to watch his older friend. Mike's age and sedentary lifestyle had taken its toll over the years. The guy's face was beet red and he was sweating. The hill wasn't all that steep. Shaking his head, he replied, "Nope, you made a good call. You said wait and see if there's any more yelling." He shrugged, his eyebrows furrowed. "I do wonder what the scream was all about.

Mike waved his fingers. "Maybe one of them saw a spider or something because they looked fine an hour or so later when they came out of the place."

"Not totally fine. The place must be getting to them. Why else would one of them carry a butcher' knife?" Adam ignored the remark about the spider. It was probably something much worse than a bug considering where they were staying. He was dreading what would happen later, on the last night that the women were there. He didn't need his sixth sense to know that today and tonight had a possibility of real peril. After all it was that dead woman Dara's birthday, and according to what Mr. Wilson, the lawyer, said, it was *the day* she wanted her friends to be at the stupid resort.

Ahead of them the trees started to thin out, and the land didn't slope nearly so much. They would soon be leaving the cover of the forest. The spires of the hotel rose above the trees, letting him know they were close. He slowed down and Mike caught up, placing his hand on Adam's arm to halt any further progress.

"We need to stay under cover but skirt around to see the front of the hotel and the lake. They might still be outside. We lost sight of them when they went into that wooded area. The lawyer wanted us to keep watch but only let them know we're here if they run into trouble."

Adam snorted. "They were in trouble the minute they stepped foot on that property."

"They don't have to stay. They could get in that car and leave any time. But they'd lose a sizeable chunk of money according to Wilson."

Adam looked over at the lined face of the retired detective. "Money isn't worth risking your life for." And he should know. A couple months ago he'd had that choice laid at his feet. He could have gone along with that demon's plans. Untold riches and power could have been his. But he could never have lived with the consequences. Things had gotten deadly enough fighting the succubus.

But that was in the past. The immediate problem was safeguarding those three women. "When it gets dark I'm going to get close to the house. I know it's bad but how bad? I'll need to touch the building to get a clearer reading on what's going on. I wish I had that necklace thing they found in the river. It had to be left by their dead friend. What did she face the night she drowned?"

Mike started off again changing course to keep to the trees. "If it comes to that later tonight, we go in." He looked over his shoulder at Adam. "And as far as touching stuff to get a genuine 'feel' for the place...well, that's why you're here, lad."

Chapter TWENTY-SIX

WHEN THE THREE WOMEN EMERGED from the path through the woods and had a clear view of the lake and hotel in the distance, Becky breathed a sigh of relief. From the way their shadows appeared to stretch beside them she'd judge the time to be close to four p.m. Exploring the grounds and being in those dreadful woods had taken longer than she'd thought.

"What now?" Cindy folded her arms over her chest and looked at each of them. "What about this altar? We've found it, so now what?"

Becky nodded. "Yeah. We've only got another few hours before we start to lose the light." She turned to Melanie. "Should we go back to the lake and look for any clues as to what she wants us to do? That's where Dara directed you first."

Melanie slipped the necklace from her pocket and held it in her hands, rubbing the gold locket as she stood silently. Finally, she spoke. "I keep hoping to channel Dara, but at this point I'm coming up blank." Her smile was sad when she looked at both of her friends. "We're all soaked to the skin from being in the forest. I say we go back inside to get changed. We've found the necklace, and now we've found the altar and that black-magic, sorcery crap."

"I can't help but wonder about that thing you saw, Mel?" Cindy looked over at Mel as they began the trek across the grounds to get to the hotel.

Melanie shook her head softly. "I really thought it was her. But it's this place. It was a trick, some evil spirit trying to separate us. Maybe Dara's father or grandfather? Who knows?"

Becky wasn't sure what Mel had seen but in that place, anything was possible. The place felt wrong.

Mel's eyes narrowed. "That clearing with the altar was a gathering place and maybe still is...if you ask me." She swept her arm around, taking in the area. "All the ghosts and spirits that are here—that's where they get together. I'm positive. Maybe at one time more than small animals were sacrificed there. I mean, there's a real evil vibe at that altar."

Becky felt her chest tighten at Mel's words. "Human sacrifice? Is what you're saying?" When Mel gave a short nod, she gasped. "Oh my God, that can't be true. This is America! They can't get away with that kind of stuff. Even back then in the fifties."

Cindy shook her head. "Powerful people get away with crap all the time."

True.

"Hang on a second," Melanie said. "I just thought of something. If you lost your life because of these Satanists, you could still be lingering here and maybe not from choice either. They may be trapped. Innocent souls trapped in an afterlife existence tied to this place."

Cindy grabbed Mel's arm, stopping her cold, "The altar. Dara was about to tell us something in her message about the altar. What if the altar's the reason that spirits or ghosts are trapped here? If it's destroyed, they become free. Does that make any sense? Could Dara have found out all of this and tried to free them?"

As Becky listened a sinking dread crept through her chest. What Mel and Cindy were speculating on was probably true. "That would be like Dara, wouldn't it?" she said. "She despised injustice. She wouldn't buy clothes she felt was made through child or slave labor. And righting the horrible wrongs here would be right up her alley...even if it cost her, her life."

Cindy sighed. "I don't know about you two, but I'm having a stiff drink after I get out of these clothes."

Melanie went to open the door, but Cindy stepped ahead blocking her. "The leaves I tucked into the doorjamb are still there. No one's been here."

"Of course not. What we're facing doesn't need to open doors. They go *through* them." Melanie shook her head before following Cindy into the resort.

When Becky stepped inside her eyes darted all around the room. But even though everything looked the same as when they'd left it, things had changed. Knowing that there was that black magic spot in the forest where innocent sacrifices might have occurred, made the shadows clinging to the corners in the large reception room take on a sinister hue of darkness. She was mentally and physically wrung out from being there. Her nerves felt like a cheese grater had sliced them raw. She headed toward the kitchen. "I'll take that drink now. Changing my clothes can wait."

Melanie nodded and started toward the kitchen with Cindy close behind. They could all use a stiff drink after being outside.

When Becky stepped into the kitchen, her jaw dropped and a cold horror filled her chest. The place had been ransacked. Food had been tossed out of the fridge and cabinets. Every drawer and door gaped wide, and the faucet hissed a steady stream of water. Broken plates and glasses lay everywhere, from the countertops to crushing bread and milk on the floor.

"'GET OUT" was written on the walls in ketchup.

"What the hell?" Melanie looked around the room, holding her hands to her cheeks.

"Shit!" Cindy screamed, glaring at the mayhem. She waded through the debris on the floor, kicking everything in her path so that they flew to the side.

She stopped at the open fridge and grabbed a bottle of vodka from the shelf in the door. "We might have to drink this straight from the bottle seeing as how all the glasses are busted." She spied a few mugs on the floor which aside from missing handles were still intact. "You missed these, shithead!" She yelled looking up and around the room.

Becky looked over at Melanie and then they stared at Cindy. She wasn't shook up, but boy oh boy, was she pissed, a grimace tightening her face.

Cindy grabbed the mugs and shoved the debris from the counter before setting them down. Her auburn hair hung loose with stray bits of twigs and leaves caught there. With the cut on her forehead, the mud on her ass and shirt, she looked totally deranged.

Becky watched Cindy's determined grin as she poured them all a healthy drink. This whole situation was beyond absurd. Her mouth clapped shut and before she knew it, her lips twitched into a smile. A chuckle burst forth from her throat as she stared at Cindy calmly handing the mugs of vodka to them as if she were hosting a party rather than standing like a harridan in the complete maelstrom that was now the kitchen.

She looked over at Mel whose lips were also curling into a smile.

Cindy lifted her mug and clinked it against Mel's and Becky's. "To Dara! If she weren't dead already, I'd kill her for bringing us here."

That was all it took for the three of them to break out into hysterical laughter, holding their sides and kicking the food and plates across the room.

Melanie finished the toast raising her mug, "Fuck you, Saul Zuckerman! Dara was better than you!"

"IS BETTER!"

Becky jumped and the grin left her face. Oh my God. She looked at Cindy and Mel. Their faces were a mixture of horror and awe. They'd heard it too. It was her voice! Dara had spoken.

Holy shit.

Chapter TWENTY-SEVEN

"OH MY GOD!" Melanie's eyes filled with tears looking around the kitchen, searching for any sign of their friend. She looked at Becky and Cindy. "You heard that too, didn't you? It wasn't just me."

"No! I heard it. Dara! We're here for you. Just let us know what you need us to do!" Cindy's eyes looked wild as she looked around the room.

Becky's heart raced so fast she thought she'd pass out. Grasping the edge of the counter for support, she whispered, "That's not possible. Yet..."

"See! I told you!" Practically vibrating with excitement, the grin on Mel's face stretched from ear to ear. "And it was after I insulted her father. She *knew* about the rituals and that altar. Somehow, she'd made that discovery. She wanted to restore the resort but she also wanted to do the right thing. That was definitely our Dara."

"We have to do this séance! Let's start it now." Cindy gulped the rest of her vodka and set the mug down with a thud on the counter.

"No. It needs to be done at night. Besides, for Dara to actually speak to us like that, had to have taken a lot of her energy. She needs to rest and we need to prepare for it. Don't forget we need to be ready but cautious." Melanie looked around the kitchen, "I say we get out of these damp clothes and then eat. We don't need plates and cutlery. I saw a frozen pizza in the freezer earlier today."

Becky was still trying to digest the fact that she'd heard Dara's voice. "Hang on a minute. We're really going to do this séance tonight? Look around you. Whatever has been messing with us, is still here. That forest was evil and creepy but it's in here too!" She pointed to the words on the wall, the ketchup hanging in thick drools. "Get Out."

Cindy looked over at the dire red message and her jaw tightened. "The only ones who have to leave are those evil spirits. Dara started this and we need to finish it."

Melanie smiled. "She reminded us that she's here, and that she's better than what we're facing. She also said she'd help us. We have to have faith that she will."

Cindy stepped over to Becky and looked into her eyes. "Becky, we need you to stretch. This is some crazy shit that we're dealing with, I'll grant you that. But you've seen and heard too much to deny that this is real. Dara knew it would take the three of us to do this. She had a premonition of her death and set this up for us to finish for her. I only wish she'd contacted us to help her sooner. She might still be alive. We need you, Becks."

Stretch? Becky sighed. That's all that she'd been doing since she walked into this to this madhouse. This night might finish them off like what had happened to Dara. Was the money worth it? Was their friendship with the dead woman worth it?

Melanie joined Cindy, her eyes leveled at Becky. "You owe her, Becky. We all do. She was always there for us at school. We might have quit, starved for funds during the last semester each year if not for her. Thanks to her we made it, and we all did well for ourselves when we graduated."

Becky nodded. It was true. Even with loans and part-time jobs it had been brutal. Dara had seen them over the rough spots. "Okay. But please tell me that you know what you're doing, Mel. I'm scared."

It was the icebreaker they all needed. Cindy smiled. "Think I'm not? Or Mel? This is what bravery looks like, Becky. Knowing the risks and doing it anyway."

"Let's go get changed." Mel smiled at her. "We'll all feel better once we're dry and filled with pizza. We can do this."

Becky set her mug of vodka down and followed them out of the kitchen. Things were still tumbling helter-skelter in her head. Since when had Melanie become the strong one or Cindy so unselfish? The roles they'd fallen into in college had reversed. Except for Dara. She'd tried to do the right thing and had died. Now it was Dara who needed their help.

But what was more unsettling was that Melanie was running the show with Cindy as backup. Compared to them she was small and helpless, instead of the sensible peacemaker. She didn't like this new realignment of relationships. At all.

***

When they got to the room, Melanie lifted her suitcase onto the bed and opened it. "It's always a good thing to purify and protect yourself before you do a séance." She pulled out a purple bag and emptied the contents onto the bed.

Becky and Cindy edged closer to see what was there. A thick, white candle, a quartz crystal on a silver chain, a bunch of dried herbs and a jar of white crystals lay on the blue comforter.

Cindy lifted the jar. "Epsom salts?" She peered over at Melanie who nodded.

"We each need to bathe with salt. That's the purify-and-protect part."

"Are you kidding? I was knocked unconscious when I took a shower earlier." Cindy tossed the jar back onto the bed. "I think I'll take a pass."

Melanie picked up the jar. "Not an option. If we're going to do this you need to bathe in salt water. I'll pour a bath and go first." She walked into the bathroom leaving the door wide open behind her.

The sound of water hissing into the tub followed before Melanie came out again. She grabbed fresh clothes and started for the bathroom again. "Grab your things and come on. We stick together. Especially after what happened to Cindy."

Becky rummaged in her bag and found a pair of track pants and a sweat shirt. She hurried into the bathroom and stood next to Cindy at the vanity. Across the room Melanie shucked her clothes and slipped into the tub.

"So, I *get* the candle and even the salt, but what's with the crystal and dried herbs?" Cindy looked over at Mel who was slipping the scrunchy from her hair, letting it flow loose over her shoulders.

"The crystal is actually a pendulum. We ask Dara questions and how it swings lets us know the answer." Melanie slipped lower in the tub letting her head fall back into the water. When she sat up again, she looked over at them. "The bundle of herbs is actually sweet grass and sage which I'll burn to smudge the room and discourage bad spirits from entering." She gestured for the towel hanging from the bar.

Cindy stepped over to hand it to her. "So, no Ouija board? Just this pendulum thing?"

Melanie stood up and wrapped herself in the towel before pulling the plug to empty the tub. Her face was tight when she turned to Cindy. "I don't like Ouija. I've tried it and never had good experiences with it. It opens too wide a portal; anything can get through."

Becky turned to look at the outline of the message that Dara had left earlier on the mirror. "Hopefully, she'll tell us more. She tried with this message but didn't finish. Maybe Cindy's right about destroying the altar, but how? You saw it, it's thick stone."

Cindy came over and joined her while Melanie got dressed. "Maybe prayer? I don't know. I gave up going to church a long time ago. So, if it comes to that, we may be out of luck."

Becky's mouth twitched. "Afraid, I'm not going to be much help in that department either. Ask Mel. We had a conversation about stuff like that last night."

Behind them, Melanie was already pouring the next bath. She came over and put her hand on Becky's shoulder, "Hopefully Dara can shed some light on what we do next. It's your turn now to bathe."

"Yeah. And here's hoping it's Dara who answers, not those other things." Becky walked over to the tub and began peeling the damp and muddy clothes off. She also hoped that Mel was experienced enough with this stuff to actually know what she was talking about. Salt and sage in the face of what they'd seen and experienced earlier didn't sound like much of a weapon. Or defense.

Chapter TWENTY-EIGHT

IT TURNED OUT THAT NONE OF THEM HAD MUCH OF AN APPETITE when they sat down with their pizza. Even Cindy who normally would eat at least three slices barely nibbled a few bites. And conversation had ceased, each of them feeling the weight of the session facing them.

Becky took a sip of water scanning Cindy's and Mel's faces. Gone was the ballsy banter of Cindy insulting whatever entity—Saul Zuckerman or whomever—that she'd done earlier. Even Mel was quiet, no lamenting about Dara or missing her or even explaining the nuances of a séance.

The light in the room had faded along with the day. Now the only illumination was the chandelier hanging above them. They'd locked the doors in the kitchen and reception area again, securing them with chairs wedged under the handles, although the menace was not outside but rather inhabiting these very walls.

Cindy sighed and then stood up, gathering the almost intact pizza and the napkins. "Anyone want anything else? More water?"

Becky shook her head. "When are we going to start this?"

"In an hour or so I think. I'd like it to be fully dark out. But I can do the smudging while we wait." Melanie reached for the bundle next to her and pulled a lighter from her pocket.

Cindy paused watching her apply the flame to the dried herbs. "Should you have an ashtray under that?"

Melanie blew the flame out, and the ends of the bundle glowed orange, an acrid smoke filling the air above the table. Her smile was wan when she rose. "What does it matter? It's not like anyone is ever going to be here again. We're going to finish this tonight." She set her mouth. "For once and for all."

"You've got a point." Cindy left to take the food refuse to the kitchen.

Melanie began with the door and then slowly made her way around the room, waving the bundle through the air constantly. "Dara, if you're here right now, we welcome you." Her words came out like a cadence; she'd done this before. "We're cleansing this room with this smudge for you. Other spirits are not welcome."

Becky sat ramrod straight in her chair watching Melanie repeat this chant as she moved around the room. Even though Mel's voice was low and hypnotic and her movements slow, with every step she took, the time before the séance would start became shorter. Becky forced herself to take a few measured breaths to calm herself.

She shot a look at Cindy when she felt their hands join at the fingers. Cindy was forcing a smile of encouragement even though her eyes were wide with apprehension.

Melanie finished the circuit of the room and then doused the burning embers in her glass of water. She lit the candle and then walked over to turn the chandelier off. Immediately the room became dim, the corners of the room engulfed in deep shadow. Although it was the same lighting as they'd had the night before, it was heavy with dread now.

"A circle of salt and then we'll begin." Melanie took the bag of sea salt which she'd brought from the kitchen and poured a thick line in a rough circle starting behind her chair and extending around the table before taking her seat.

Becky couldn't stop her knees from trembling so she pressed them tight together before edging forward in her chair. This was it. There was no backing out now.

"Take my hand, Cindy, and then hold Becky's hand."

Becky felt Cindy's whole hand close over hers. She was about to reach for Melanie's but Melanie shook her head. Instead, with her free hand she held the end of the chain high, so that the crystal hung an inch or so above the table. The flame of the candle flickered in one of the prisms of the glass as it dangled there, swaying and twisting slightly.

"By the power of light and goodness we call only benign spirits to come forward. Dara Zuckerman, if you are here, we wish to communicate with you. Please give us a sign that you are here. Swing the pendulum toward me to indicate yes."

Melanie felt Cindy's fingers grasp hers a little harder as she watched for any movement in the crystal. Melanie's hand wavered a bit but the crystal fob stayed perfectly still. It was so quiet that she could hear Cindy's and Mel's breathing. The next few seconds crept by, feeling more like minutes as all three of them waited for any movement.

When Mel spoke again, Becky jerked. "Dara. You asked us here to be with you on your birthday. We came. Please let us know that you are also here with us now."

Again the crystal was still, the only movement being a slight waver from Melanie's arm. Becky's gaze flitted around the room. She couldn't help feeling that there was something else with them, watching them silently.

She jerked when the candle flared bright, leaping higher and bending to the side for a moment. Becky's lips parted, and her breath froze in her chest watching it. There was no physical reason for that to happen, no drafts or air disturbance to cause it.

The crystal began swaying, a little at first becoming faster and swinging back and forth, closer and closer to Melanie's chest. Melanie's eyes glittered when she glanced at Becky and Cindy. "She's here."

"Ask her about that altar. What else did she mean to tell us about it?" Cindy's cheeks glowed where the candle light highlighted next to her parted lips.

Melanie hissed at Cindy, "We have to ask questions where there's a yes or no response. It's a limitation of the pendulum, but I'll take that any day over a Ouija board."

Becky ventured a question. "Are you trapped here, Dara. Is it that altar and...sorcery place in the woods?" She watched the crystal but Melanie jumped in, her voice sharp.

"I'm asking the questions. Only one of us can be the leader, and you both know I've got more experience." Melanie shot a dark look at Becky, before she pared down to the question, "Are you trapped here, Dara?"

The crystal began moving in a circle and then swayed back and forth, swinging toward Melanie.

"That's a yes, right?" Cindy's eyes were wide when she looked Mel and then her gaze became riveted again on the movement of the crystal.

"Yes. She's telling us she's here. Trapped in this place." Mel was silent for a few moments as the crystal became still again. "How can we help you?" She shook her head and corrected the question so Dara would be able to give a yes or no. "Is it the altar holding you here?"

The crystal began arcing in a circle, around and around in a six-inch sphere.

"What's that mean, Mel? What's she saying?" Cindy edged back a little as if afraid the sweep of the glass would become bigger and actually hit her.

Becky felt it too. She didn't like the fact it was getting faster and wilder in its arc. Even the flame of the candle reacted, burning lower and almost flickering out.

"She's not answering. Either she doesn't know or—"

The cut glass in the chandelier above them tinkled. Becky's eyes darted up, peering at it. The chandelier shook like some unseen hand jostled the chain that held it. It became more agitated, jerking up and down and from side to side. Becky was rooted to her seat, suddenly frozen and unable to move staring at it.

Melanie's voice grew louder this time, but there was a trembling note of fear in it. "Other spirits, any spirits besides Dara's, you are not welcome here. Leave us!"

Oh shit! What Becky had dreaded was happening! The bad entities, the ones who had trashed the kitchen, thrown Cindy from the shower were here, in this room right now! Cindy jumped to her feet so abruptly that the chair she'd been sitting in tipped, and banged hard against the wooden floor.

"No! We need to stay connected. Sit down, Cindy." Melanie's hand shot out to tighten on Cindy's arm.

"Are you kidding? That thing's not stable." Cindy watched the chandelier dance above her, the crystal glass tinkling and bobbing in the air like a marionette controlled by an unseen hand.

Becky jerked back as well, coming to her feet. All the while the chandelier's movement became wilder, swaying and jerking so hard that the chain holding it looked like it may give way any second. Dust particles from the ceiling fell onto the table.

Suddenly an icy wind swept through the room, lifting Becky's hair from her shoulders. The candle's flame doused leaving them in total darkness. Her heart leapt in her chest, staring hard for any sign of Mel or Cindy. All the while the frigid blast blanketed her, the chandelier now thudding each time it lifted and fell down, straining the chain.

"I'll get the lights! You guys move back from the table, for God's sake!" Cindy's voice bordered on hysteria, and her feet thudded quickly across the room.

CRASH! The chandelier smashed into the table. The candle flew from the table, splattering hot wax on Becky's bare ankle, while crystal fobs clattered to the floor in every direction.

"We rebuke you!" Melanie screamed, "In the name of all that is good and pure, I command you to leave us in peace!"

In the pitch-black, the sound of wood scraping against wood was followed by a series of thuds. The cold air blowing over Becky's face and neck made it hard to breathe. She stumbled toward where she thought the door would be. All hell was breaking loose, and they had to get out of there! In the utter darkness, she ran into the wall, her head butting into it.

She shook her head to clear it, hardly even aware in the maelstrom of Cindy's curses, about the light switch or Melanie's screamed commands. Her hand brushed the frame of the door, and she felt the chair they'd wedged under the handle. She tore it loose and practically threw it.

Thuds on the wooden door almost made her heart stop.

"Let us in!" A male voice was followed by more pounding thuds.

Her fingers flipped the dead bolt and she yanked the door wide. The beam of light hit her squarely in the face before it lowered. Her mouth fell open seeing an old guy and a young man, hardly more than a teenager standing there.

"Help us! Get us out of here!" She stumbled out, clinging to the old guy's leather jacket.

The younger one pushed past her, holding a flashlight before him. "What the hell?"

Becky didn't want to but she had to see. She turned feeling the sudden quiet in the room behind her. The flashlight's beam had settled on her two friends. Cindy knelt on the floor beside Melanie.

Oh my God. A trickle of blood rolled from the corner of Mel's mouth, and her face was a dark shade. She was perfectly still. The chain and pendulum wrapped tightly around her neck.

Chapter TWENTY-NINE

ADAM RUSHED OVER to the woman on the floor. When he touched her neck he could feel her life force. It was weak but still there. The other woman had pried the chain from her throat and tipped the downed woman's head back.

"Give me some space here!" The woman pinched the blond's nose and began blowing long measured breaths into her mouth.

He sensed Mike and the other woman behind him but ignored them, placing his hands over the blond woman's heart, pumping it with a steady downward pressure.

"Is she... Oh my God, Mel!" The woman beside Mike sobbed and then fell to her knees beside him.

"She's going to be all right. She's alive." Adam could feel the woman's heart flutter under his fingers and she coughed, stopping the other woman's attempts at resuscitation.

It was all he could do to stay squatting there when every cell in his body screamed to run...run far, far away. The place felt as cold as a morgue. The sense of evil was truly terrifying. He felt yellow-green, pus-filled tendrils already lashing at his inner self. He'd encountered that kind of evil once before, and it had damn near killed him.

"Melanie! Oh God. It tried to strangle you!" The woman kneeling next to Melanie's head helped her sit up.

Melanie rubbed at her throat, and her breath was raspy peering at Adam and then up to Mike.

The other woman, the one with dark hair was kneeling beside her, stroking her head as she pinned them with narrow eyes. "I saw you. You work for that lawyer, don't you? What are you two—"

"I'm Mike and that's Adam." Mike shone the flashlight so that his face was highlighted. "Yes. Anthony Wilson hired us to keep an eye out for you three. I'd say he made a good call judging by what happened to your friend there."

"Help us? You mean *cheat* us out of the inheritance." The woman's face twisted into a hard sneer glaring up at Mike.

Adam had heard enough. These women were lucky to be alive. They had no idea what they'd stumbled upon...but he did. "We need to get you out of here. How you survived this long is—"

"No." Melanie croaked. She waved her hand cutting Adam off as raspy words tumbled out. "We're staying. We need to help Dara. Becky, open the door to the kitchen and get some light in here."

Adam grabbed his cell phone from his pocket. He clicked it on but the screen remained dark. Damn. It had been fully charged when he left this morning. It hit him then. It was this place. Somehow it had killed his cell phone. Shit, they couldn't even phone for help, let alone use his flashlight app. He reached into his back pocket for the small flashlight Mike had given him earlier in the day. When Becky spoke, he looked over at her.

"Mel! He's right. We can't control what's in this place. I knew this séance was a bad idea."

The other woman who'd helped Melanie, scowled over at the one still kneeling there. "Just get the lights, Becky. Give Mel a break for a moment and quit your whining."

"I'll get the light." Mike shone the flashlight around the room looking for a door to the kitchen. Finding it, he reached through, fumbling for a switch as he kept his flashlight shining on the others gathered on the floor.

Adam saw the shattered chandelier covering the table. He saw a candle and the bundle of sweetgrass that had been used for the smudging. He knew what those things were for and was dismayed. Damn it! They'd been doing a séance, in *this* of all places! The place was evil incarnate. Sure, there were ghosts here. He'd seen a few since he'd entered, but there were also glimpses of darker, more ominous entities that shouldn't be messed with.

A second later light spilled in from the kitchen. Mike braced the kitchen door open and came back over to them. "What the hell happened in the kitchen? It looks like a bomb went off in there."

Becky snorted. "That's nothing. We've seen a chair levitate. Something pushed Cindy out of the shower so hard she was knocked unconscious." A hysterical bray of laughter burst from her mouth. "There's even a devil worship circle in the forest!" She blinked a few times, her voice shrill. "Dara bought a real *gem* with this place!"

From the tone of her voice and tears forming in her eyes, it was obvious that Becky was on the verge of coming apart. He looked at Cindy, seeing the cut on her forehead. She started to get up and then reached for Melanie's hand to help her get to her feet. His mouth fell open watching them. These women were batshit crazy to be there!

"You won't leave despite all that's happened?" Adam had to hear it again even though he already knew the answer.

"No we're not! Dara is trapped here, and we're going to help her!" Melanie swiped at the ribbon of blood on her upper lip and then brushed it on her pants. She clung to Cindy's arm, the two of them resolute in their decision.

Adam's gaze slid past them. A pale ethereal shape of a woman wavered in the air behind the two friends. From the look in her eyes watching the two women, it was clear that this was Dara's spirit. He sighed. "She's standing right behind you, you know. She loves you for being here." He glanced at the spirit and smiled. "Happy birthday, by the way."

Melanie's eyes almost popped out on her cheekbones. "You can see her?" She started to turn but stopped when he answered.

"Yeah. That's what I do. I see spirits, and know things about people. That's why Mike asked me here. We want to *help you*, not cheat you out of your inheritance." He became distracted by the spirit's movement, her hand pointing to the pocket of Melanie's pants. He couldn't help the sinking feeling in his chest seeing her. She'd been so young and alive when she'd died. It wasn't fair.

Adam looked at Melanie. "She wants you to give me what you've got in your pocket. It's a piece of jewelry, right?"

Becky stepped over to the other women. "Don't do it. Let's end this right now. We'll make a deal with these guys. We give them some of the money in exchange for them getting us out of here. We'll come back tomorrow and meet with that lawyer. He doesn't have to know we were even gone."

The other two women just gaped at her. Cindy's head even pulled back a bit before she spoke. "This is just about the money for you, isn't it? You never really cared about Dara. Why'd you even come here, Becky? Did you know she would leave us money?"

Becky face darkened and she hissed at them, "Like it's not about the money for you, Cindy? You were the one who tried to leave and then came running back. I'm sure you were counting that money with every step you took hightailing it back here."

Adam watched Dara's spirit as the two women argued. Disappointment emanated in her face watching Becky.

"Stop it! Stop your bickering." Melanie turned on both of them, before shoving her hand in her pocket and getting the chain and locket out. "Here." She handed Adam the piece of jewelry before turning, her hand reaching out trying to feel or sense Dara's spirit.

As soon as Adam's fingers closed over the heart shape, an image flashed in his mind. A young woman, lurching as she headed for the lake in the dead of night. Anger swarmed through her like a cloud of angry bees—anger at her father. She stumbled but caught herself, weaving to the side like she was drunk or something.

His neck muscle clenched tight. Not drunk.

Poisoned.

The sound of her bare feet slapping on the wooden dock filled his head. She reached the end, swaying when she came to a stop inches from the water. Her scream reverberated across the still lake before she flung the locket away.

He gasped, feeling her sudden panic. A force like a freight train had slammed into her. Arms wind milling as she fell forward. The shock of the cold water consumed her, clearing her head, sobering her fast. Her hands pulled at the water, while her feet pushed against the silt-covered bottom of the lake.

Something held her back, would not relinquish its deadly hold on her. She kicked out, clawing at the water with her hands. Lungs burning as she thrashed in the dark water, filled with blind panic.

Cold invaded her body at her last gasp, a final silent scream. Adam staggered, his knees jelly as he gasped for breath.

"What is it, lad? Are you okay?" Mike stepped closer and put his beefy paw on Adam's shoulder.

Adam couldn't speak. More and more images flooded into his head. His fingers fisted the small locket. A pentagram, robed figures in a glade of trees carrying torches, an altar—and death.

At Mike's firm jostle of his shoulder, his mind cleared. He looked around, his gaze once more in the present. Oh God. His chest fell seeing the woman from the vision. Dara was at the forefront while many other spirits had gathered behind her. All of them looked frightened, their eyes looking around the room furtively. They were trapped here, terrified of the evil that permeated the resort.

His mouth had gone dry but he managed to whisper, "Dara? You tried to help these souls. But your enemy was too strong. You never stood a chance of beating it alone." Adam looked into the dead woman's eyes. She nodded and then her gaze fell on Melanie and Cindy and then over to Becky.

"What? What is she saying?" Melanie broke away from Cindy and grabbed the front of Adam's jacket. "Tell us!"

Becky screamed at the blond woman, "He told you! Dara never had a chance! And now we're going to die like she did!" A foam of spittle dribbled from the corner of her mouth. "We can still get the money!" She gave a wild-eyed look at Mike and Adam. "We'll cut you guys in! But we gotta get out of here! What good is the money if we're dead?"

Her words hung in the air. Adam could sense Melanie wavering, her chin lowering as the futility of their quest sunk in. Even Mike's gaze darted over the room, waiting for something to happen.

Cindy was the only one who stood taller, pulling her shoulders back glaring at Becky. She wrapped an arm over Mel's shoulders, pulling her close. "Screw that! Dara said she would help us. We have to believe that. The evil in this place must be destroyed. The fact that a kid like this showed up isn't coincidence. I'd say the odds just got evened up!"

"You're insane. We can't do this." Becky stepped over to Adam, her eyes filled with tears, "Tell them. You say you can see Dara. Why do we have to die as well?"

Adam's gaze shifted to the other two women. Cindy's eyes had softened a bit watching Becky break down in tears, covering her face with her hands.

Melanie wrapped an arm around Cindy's waist and glowered as she hissed, "Go then! You're a hypocrite, Becky! You never believed in any of this. You thought I was an idiot because I do. And now when things happen that you can't explain, you want to run away from it! No matter what happens to Dara's spirit!" She spat at the ground. "Tomorrow, you'll deny to yourself that any of this happened! No wonder Hank escapes into his research. When it comes right down to it, you're shallow and self-absorbed! You want the whole damn world to revolve around the great 'Doctor Rebecca Sloan, PhD!'" She took a breath and said, her voice low and even, "You hide it pretty good, you know that? But the fact is Becky, you only think of yourself."

Before Adam knew it, Becky spun around to face Melanie. "What do you know of me? You know nothing! I was always there for all of you, keeping the peace between you, keeping your bloody secrets!"

Adam watched as Dara approached Becky, staring with a wounded expression at the frantic woman. Her hand rose, and her ethereal fingertips grazed Becky's cheek. She looked at Adam and whispered, "*Tell her that I know her. I know her favorite color is yellow, and her middle name is Helen. I know she suspects Hank is cheating on her, which I'm sorry to say, he is.*"

Oh shit. He looked over at Mike who stared at the floor, cracking his knuckles and wishing he were anywhere else but there, in the middle of a catfight in an abandoned haunted resort. Mike didn't know the half of it.

Cindy was about to say something, but Adam raised his hand like a traffic cop silencing her. He placed his hand on Becky's arm pulling her gently so that she faced him. With just that touch he knew her fear as well as how alone she'd always felt, always on the periphery in this group of friends. "Dara feels your pain. She's here. She told me yellow is your favorite color, your middle name is Helen, and to ditch Hank. You're right about him."

Becky's mouth had fallen open as he spoke and she blinked a few times. "Dara? She told you that?"

He nodded, but it was Cindy who came forward stepping through Dara and putting her arm around Becky, "We're here for you too, Becky. I never knew how you felt. I guess maybe we always took you for granted. I mean...you always act so damn self-assured!" She took her friend by the shoulders. "It's scary to see you so damn rattled, okay? Like seeing 'Mother Hen' become all human and shit." She kissed Becky's cheek. "And if you decide to bail...well, I won't think any less of you. And I'm pretty sure Dara wouldn't either."

Adam could sense a sea of change in Becky. With just that simple touch of appreciation and affection she found her footing again. She stood up straighter, her eyes on Cindy. She was still afraid—hell, terrified, actually—who could blame her? But anger sparked in there too—at her husband and herself for turning a blind eye to his infidelity.

He was an asshole, and it took Dara to confirm that. He saw her look over to Melanie and back to Cindy as it dawned on her. These were her true friends.

Becky pulled back and looked up at Cindy. "I'm staying. Dara needs me and so do the two of you." She managed a small smile. "Besides, I'm going to need that money when I kick Hank's cheating ass out."

Melanie stepped closer, but she didn't raise a hand to comfort Becky, looking at Adam, "Now what? Has Dara told you how we're going to help her?"

Adam sighed and glanced over at Mike. The old detective looked every one of his sixty-seven years, and his face was an awful shade of pale. If they were going to stay and do this they needed to know what they were up against. They might all want to run once they knew.

"You said you saw an altar and pentagram. It was in the forest." He knew that that place was bad and that had to be why. It was some sort of satanic cult.

Melanie nodded. "Yeah. There's a clearing and all kinds of inscriptions and carvings in the altar, along with people's initials. We think Dara's father or grandfather was involved in it. Look at the picture in the locket. Dara mutilated the photo of her dad. She must have caught onto her family's history with this place."

Adam smiled seeing Dara nod her head quickly, her eyes beseeching him. He looked at Melanie. "Sure, you're not gifted too? Dara just confirmed your theory."

Again, Melanie turned searching the room for her dead friend. "Shit! I wish I could do that."

"No you don't. Trust me." Mike snorted. "He's had his share of problems because of that so-called gift."

Adam took a deep breath and continued, "We have to go out there again. We don't leave until the altar and that unholy place are destroyed. It's the only way to honor your friend and abide by her wishes." The thought of it made his knees go weak. What he wasn't saying but what was in everyone's mind was the fact that it wouldn't happen without a fight.

Chapter THIRTY

"WE'LL BURN THE WHOLE DAMN FOREST! That should do it." Cindy reached in her pocket and came out with a lighter, flicking it to a flame.

"Not gonna happen with all that rain last night. Everything's soaked," Mike said.

'*The garage. There's a sledgehammer there.*' Adam looked over at Dara's spirit when her voice sounded in his head. He turned to the three women. "You're sure you're up for this? We could wait until daylight at least."

Melanie wasn't the only one who shook her head at his suggestion. Behind her, Dara and the other ghostly bodies also showed their disagreement while Melanie voiced the reasoning. "Dara wanted us here specifically on her birthday. That's today. It's got to be done tonight."

A look at Dara confirmed this. '*Before the equinox,*' sounded in his head.

Adam turned to Mike and rolled his eyes. "We couldn't have found out about all this when it was light or like maybe yesterday? No. We've got to wait until it's night to go into a forest crawling with evil."

"We have to do this. You can't back out now. The lawyer hired you to protect us."

Adam grimaced countering Cindy's words. "We will. Doesn't mean I have to like it though." He started walking across the room to the door, shining the light before him. "C'mon. There's a sledgehammer in the garage. Grab anything else in there that we can use to destroy that pentagram and altar."

Behind him, Cindy added her two cents. "If there's a can with any gas, I'm still voting for fire."

"I'll be sayin' a few prayers. Never was a religious guy until I took up with this lad," Mike muttered taking up the rear as they walked out into the night. "Up till now the only 'Hail Mary's' I've been saying is when it's the ninth inning and the Yankees are down by one run!" He made a sick smile at his weak attempt at humor.

Stepping out the front entrance, Adam shone the light over the set of stairs so that the others would see their way. The moon was hidden behind a bank of clouds that scudded fast across the sky. A scan with his flashlight showed the garage off to the left, about fifty feet away, the large metal door hanging open.

He was about to turn to see how the women were doing behind him when a loud banging in the garage made him jump.

"What the hell? Was that a gunshot?" Cindy stepped closer to him, pulling Melanie along beside her.

"I don't think so." Adam held the flashlight before him aiming it once more at the garage. The beam showed the door now shut tight. A ripple of fear shot through his shoulders seeing it, knowing that the dark power was present. It had banged that door shut to keep them out.

"How are we going to get in there now?"

It was Melanie who answered Becky's question. "Dara will help us. She said she would. We can't let them scare us."

Adam hoped the blond woman was right. His grip on the flashlight tightened as he strode forward. If he hesitated even for a moment, he'd feed the evil with his fear. It was already too powerful, unchallenged for years and years claiming this dilapidated resort. "We'll get in even if we have to break the door down."

He looked over at the three women. "You trust your friend to help, and you have to keep that faith no matter what happens. We have to be cautious but that doesn't mean be afraid. That's what these entities prey on."

Mike stepped up beside him, the five of them walking shoulder to shoulder. The old man frowned but his feet never faltered. "Watch your step. The ground's pretty rough." He shone his light before them.

When a small spark of light appeared to his right Adam saw that Cindy had the cigarette lighter in hand, the flame wavering as she swept in low to see the walkway. After a few steps it went out and she yelped, "Damn! I'll have to let it cool before I try that again."

The garage loomed darkly before them. Adam handed Melanie his light and pushed at the door but as he'd expected it wouldn't budge. He braced his feet before ramming his shoulder against it. It squeaked and gave a little but then clamped shut again with a snap. It was like there was a force behind it, pushing it closed. Which of course there was.

"Let me help you." Mike joined him. "On the count of three. One. Two. Three."

The two of them thudded their shoulders hard against the door and then almost fell onto an old tractor when it suddenly gave way.

"You did it!" Melanie shone the light stepping inside after them. She aimed the light to the right revealing the old workbench and layers of cobwebs.

"I've been in here. There's nothing on that workbench except boxes and old car parts. Shine the light farther back, Mel," Becky whispered.

Adam's gaze followed the beam past the tractor and to the far wall. A rake and wheelbarrow were tucked in the corner but beside it leaning against the wall was an iron crowbar and sledgehammer. He took the flashlight from Melanie and started for them, brushing by the old tractor. He could hear Mike's labored breathing behind him. The place was stuffy and thick with the scent of decay.

"What else is there? Do you see a gas can or anything we can make into a torch?" Cindy called out.

She had a good point. They only had the two flashlights, and if the batteries died, they'd only have the moonlight to see by. And from the looks of that forest, not even beams of sunlight would penetrate the thick canopy of trees. Mike grabbed the crowbar, and Adam turned the light to the other side of the building. But aside from wooden boxes and a few old tires there didn't look to be too much there.

"What about that rake? We could break it in two, but we'd need some cloth soaked in kerosene or gas to tie around it?"

Mike answered Cindy, "That could work. But I don't see anything flammable, definitely no gas or we'd get a whiff of it."

"Olive or corn oil could work. There's some in the kitchen. And dish towels. You get the rake, and Cindy and I will go back to the kitchen to get the other stuff." Melanie started back, but Adam's voice rang out, stopping her cold.

"No. We stick together. We'll bring what we need but you two aren't going back in there alone." He shone the light over the wall where the big hammer rested and grabbed it. He saw Mike feel his way to the corner and get the rake.

Mike stepped into the beam of light, pushing by the old tractor again. "Let's get out of here. This shed gives me the heeby-jeebies. I thought the resort had a bad vibe, but this place is worse." He looked over to Adam. "You know it's gotta be bad when a regular guy like me is able to sense it."

"Welcome to my world," Adam replied, heading for the entrance. When he stepped outside he inhaled deeply. The garage had been stale and the air difficult to breathe. The darkness inside had been oppressive—a darker kind of dark. But one good thing was that the moon was out. Even if it was the last half of it, it cast enough light that the walkway was visible now.

Becky led the way this time up the flagstone path to the front of the resort. "Actually, it's easier to get to the forest from the kitchen anyway. Just as well we're going back in to make some torches."

"Great." Mike's voice dripped with sarcasm. "That's going to make it all *sooo* much easier." There was a small flash of light and then he announced, "By my watch it's about ten o'clock. We've got two hours to make this happen if we want to be finished before that equinox you were talking about, Melanie."

Two hours. Getting the stuff from the garage had been relatively easy once they managed to get the door open. Adam wasn't sure that was a good thing. Maybe the dark forces they were up against had regrouped, protecting the evil temple in the forest.

Cindy looked over her shoulder at them before going up the steps to the front door. "That's not much time. We still have to make these torches or we're never going to be able to find the spot in the forest. We kind of stumbled on it this afternoon."

"You didn't have Adam with you. Trust me, he'll find it without these torches." Mike stepped through the door.

Even before Adam entered, he felt the emptiness in there. No sign of Dara or the other spirits when he looked over to where they'd been gathered. His heart beat faster, and he hurried after the others going into the kitchen. A celestial, spiritual storm was brewing that would break when they reached the satanic altar in the woods.

For the first time in a long while he fingered the tourmaline stone that he wore on a loop of leather around his neck. A wise and powerful psychic had given it to him for protection. He wished she were there to help him again. He would need that protection as well as a fair amount of luck.

The women were busy soaking rags, while Mike angled the handle of the rake against this knee to crack it in two. He looked at the total mess of dishes and cutlery and the message on the wall.

The back door in the kitchen swayed open slowly on its own. Outside was darkness and the heavy presence of the forest. The hair on the back of his neck spiked high watching the door open even wider. Whatever evil was out there now taunted them, inviting them to its lair.

Chapter THIRTY-ONE

BECKY STEELED HERSELF for what lay ahead. Going into the garage again had been scary but going into that creepy forest—again!—would take every ounce of courage and then some.

One by one they stepped out of the kitchen into the night, pausing on the stone patio while Cindy lit the torches. "We made one for each of us to carry." She smirked. "That broom came in handy after all. It makes great torches."

"Good thinking." Adam grabbed his and set off across the patio to the path.

Each step Becky took felt like her feet were wading through porridge, cold sticky porridge. She looked over at Cindy. "Do you feel it too? It's like whatever is out there is making walking harder."

Behind her, Melanie answered, "I feel it in my stomach. Even though I didn't eat much, it feels like a lump of lead in there."

It was true. Whether it was fear or nerves or the malice hanging heavy in the air, Becky's gut churned like she could be sick at any moment.

"Just breathe," Adam said. "Take slow measured breaths to center yourself." He then turned to Mike. "That goes for you too, old man."

Mike huffed a sigh. "It's hard to do that at the best of times. Should have quit smoking years ago."

In the light of the moon, Becky saw the forest about ten feet ahead of them. There was no sound in the air, no crickets or any sign of life. There was just the low hiss of the oil in the torches burning, breaking the stillness.

As she stepped onto the slippery path, she felt the evil of the place prickle her skin. A heaviness weighed in her chest when she entered, while the brush on either side of the path clawed like tentacles to ensnare her.

Melanie darted forward to whisper to Adam, "We walked for about ten minutes till we came upon it. Do you see Dara or any spirits in here?"

"No. But they weren't in the resort either when we went back inside." Adam held the torch higher, lighting only a foot or so of the path ahead. The trees seemed to capture his voice along with any light that might have been there from the moon.

"So, you think they're in here?" Melanie persisted, her concern for Dara evident.

"Hey!" Cindy's shout was followed by the sound of her feet thudding and the crack of a twig breaking.

Becky turned but Mike had beat her to Cindy, holding her arm.

"What happened?" Even Mike was whispering.

"Someone pushed me! I didn't trip. Shit! Why are they always pushing *me*? Never Mel or Becky!" Cindy's footsteps squished in the mud of the path while she muttered some ripe curses.

Becky turned to follow Melanie and Adam again. She held the torch low, her heart beating hard with each step forward. Forget about keeping her breathing even, it was hard to not gulp air it was so heavy and cold. It felt like climbing a mountain.

"Hold up."

She looked ahead past Melanie where Adam held his torch high, illuminating the pale bark of a birch tree. *That* birch tree. This was the spot where Cindy had fallen, and they'd gone off the trail to find her knife. Now the tree seemed to glow like a sentinel in the dark forest, the border into a den of evil pestilence.

They were there.

Oh God. Her chest grew tight, and her heart felt like it would explode thudding hard against her ribs. She jumped when Mike eased by her, holding the iron crowbar in his hand.

Adam stepped off the path and Mike followed closely. She could hear twigs snapping under their feet even though the undergrowth was thick muffling the sound a bit.

She waited a moment for Melanie to step after the two men but she stood rooted to the spot. She met Melanie's wide eyed, deer-in-the-headlights gaze, feeling exactly the same way. Hell, she'd been ready to run earlier. It looked like Mel needed some time to bolster her nerve.

"We'll be okay, Mel. Stay behind me, and Cindy's got your back. Follow me." As much as she hated doing this, she entered the thicket of trees. They were friends, and they needed to stick together. This was for Dara.

Adam's voice carried through the brush, filled with shock and dread. "Holy shit, this place is *bad*!" They heard the sound of the crowbar striking stone.

Cindy grabbed her arm and pulled them both forward, shoving branches out of the way with her other hand. "Did you find it?"

The instant Cindy stepped on one of the flagstones, she was swept into the air. "Umph!" she grunted. She let out a piercing scream as she slammed into the side of a tree, a broken branch skewering her by the shoulder, holding her. Her feet jerked, suspended from the ground and she dropped the torch. She scrabbled at the bloody branch stump, screaming in agony.

Becky raced to the tree holding her torch high. She stared in horror before she managed to get out a yell, "Help! Cindy's been stabbed!"

"What?" It was the old man thundering back through the thicket of trees. "Oh shit!" A crash of branches was followed by a sickening thud.

"Mike?" Adam's voice came through the brush.

Becky turned to call out again, but her words were silenced in the sudden wind that buffeted her face. It screeched through the boughs overhead, raining down leaves and pine cones. At the loud crack overhead, her gaze flew to the spot above her.

Suddenly she was knocked to the side, falling on the ground. A blinding pain cleaved her head before everything went black.

Chapter THIRTY-TWO

ADAM TRIED TO GET TO MIKE FIRST. The old guy was down, laying in the brush while the gale-force wind shook the forest. Every step felt like he was pushing a wall, barely managing to stay upright, fending off the swirling branches and debris with his arm. Finally, he reached him, and scuttled lower to squat next to him.

"Mike! Are you—"

"It's my heart kid! My chest is on fire... I can't..." His eyes rolled up, and his head fell back onto the ground.

"Oh shit! No!" Tears filled his eyes while his hands pushed at Mike's chest, over his heart. Mike was alive. He almost toppled over onto the barrel chest of his friend, tears trickling down his cheeks, but this time from relief. But Mike needed help—fast.

He got up and stumbled, trying to make his way in the whirlwind of branches and leaves toward the women. What had happened? He knew what was causing this, that wasn't in question. But what had the beast in these woods done to the women?

His mouth dropped in horror seeing Cindy impaled on the tree. But she was moving, trying to pull forward off the spike, her face a mask of agony. He lurched forward to her and almost fell on Becky's still form laying on the ground. She wasn't moving at all. He bent and felt her neck, checking for a pulse. He breathed a quick sigh of relief. She was alive. These were things he'd normally know with a glance, seeing their auras, but this was anything but normal in the forest. All hell had broken loose when Mike had slammed the crowbar into that altar.

Where was the other woman? Melanie? He stood up and tried to see through the trees. The wind had doused all light but still he should be able to *'feel'* her presence. But there was nothing.

"Melanie! Where are you? If you're nearby, you have to leave! Go for help!" He waited a few moments but the railing windstorm was the only thing he heard in answer. Shit! They would all die if he didn't stop this!

A cold fury filled him, and he gripped the handle of the heavy hammer with everything he had.

"By God, you won't win! This ends tonight!" He careened through the underbrush, beaten and shaken like a leaf in the maelstrom. Inch by inch he made his way to the clearing. The flagstones of the circle were like treading on a living force field, vibrating and shaking from the ancient evil power of the site. When he looked down a river of blood flowed between the slabs, slaking his sneakers, making every step slick and slippery.

A blast of icy air hit him, knocking him to the ground. His hip took the impact and pain raced like a searing bullet through his body. He tried to rise but it hurt too much. He could see the altar only five feet away. He had to get there—had to destroy the damn thing to stop this madness.

His blood ran cold when he saw the dark, robed figure materialize before him standing between him and the altar. Its eyes glowed red like burning embers in the dark cowl surrounding it. A bellow like an angry bull split his eardrums. A cloud of dust and debris hit him squarely in the face, blinding him. He swiped at his face while his eyes burned from the grit he'd been hit with.

"You sick son of a bitch! You don't belong here! I'm going to destroy you. Starting with that damn altar." His eyes shut tight from the grit being flung at him like a zillion pebbles, Adam pulled himself forward.

His fingers closed around his tourmaline stone and he said a silent prayer. The head of the sledgehammer caught between the stones behind him and he was forced to yank at it to loosen it. Every movement caused an arc of pain to flare in his hip.

The wind increased, and he found himself gulping bursts of air into his lungs. But he was edging forward even so. Just a little bit farther. But he had to get by that thing, that creature. And then what? He couldn't even stand let alone swing the hammer hard enough to bust that slab of stone.

His knuckles went numb when he pulled his body forward. He didn't have to *see* to know that he was there. His hand pressed into cold as frigid as ice, emanating from the specter. He felt another presence beside him.

'Now Adam!' echoed in his mind. The icy coldness vanished and his pain eased. Not waiting for anything more to happen, he pushed his body up from the stones. He stood still as a statue for a moment. *'Hurry! I can't hold it off for long!'* What the hell? The cold and wind had vanished as quickly as it had started. He was still blind, his eyes tearing up trying to shed the grime coating them, but every cell in his body was ready for what he had to do.

He gripped the sledgehammer, staggering from the weight of it. He was weak as a kitten.

'Here, hon.' He felt a hand lay over his. *'Let's do this!'* He managed to raise the hammer above his head, and using every ounce of energy in his body he smashed at the stone.

The thud jarred through his arms, rippling to his very core. The pain in his hip soared, but he forced himself to ignore it. Again and again, he hammered at that stone, invoking the power of light to aid him.

"Dara? Is that you? I can't see!"

'Don't worry hon, you will. Keep going!'

At the tenth swing he fell to the side, spent and ready to pass out from the pain. Just one more. He lifted the heavy mallet and banged it on the stone. He shuddered, and as he fell, he heard and felt the wrenching crack and thud of the altar splitting apart.

The slippery stones once more met him when he fell. But this time the pain was no more. Only peaceful blackness.

Chapter THIRTY-THREE

A THROBBING PAIN in her head woke Becky. It pounded like a jackhammer with every beat of her heart. Her eyes saw a pink haze before she opened them, squinting at the sunlight threading through the canopy of leaves.

Oh God. It came back to her in a nightmarish rush what had happened. Cindy! She gaped at the tree where Cindy was impaled. But she was gone? A quick look around showed the reddish curls of the other woman spread among the leaves and branches strewn around. As she sat up fresh pain shot through her.

Cindy lay on the ground a few feet away. How did she get off the tree? But there was no time for that. She scrambled quickly over to her friend. A sigh of relief eased out when she saw Cindy's eyes twitch. She was alive! "Cindy!"

The sweatshirt Cindy wore was stiff with the blood from her wound but none of it looked wet and fresh. She wasn't bleeding anymore.

Cindy moaned. Her eyes fluttered a few times and then opened. "Oh God. I hurt so bad." She lifted her head and looked around. "What happened? Did Adam manage to break the stone altar?" Her eyes opened wider when she looked at Becky, her gaze riveted to the side of Becky's head. "You're hurt too."

Becky nodded and another wave of pain at the movement almost made her gag. "A branch fell. It hit my head and that's the last thing I know."

She had to see about the others. Melanie, Adam, and Mike. They might not have made it. She pushed herself up from the ground. "Stay here."

Cindy sighed. "Don't worry. It hurts too much to move. I can't believe I'm even alive."

Becky agreed but she didn't say it. After being stabbed through and through with a tree branch, she should be dead. It must have just missed her lung. But how the hell had she gotten down from the tree?

Stumbling, her head throbbing with every step, Becky made her way through the thicket of trees. Mike lay off to the side, his mouth open and snoring softly. What had happened to him? There was no blood or anything visibly wrong. She continued walking until she came to the edge of the small circle of flagstones.

Adam lay in a heap on the stones, the sledgehammer next to him. Another step closer and she could see the two parts of the altar laying in a 'V'.

He'd done it!

But at what price? She hurried forward and then knelt, placing her fingers on his neck to check for a pulse. He jerked and then his eyes flew open.

"What?" He turned his head to see the altar. "We did it." His fingers felt the stones next to him and he sat up. "Mike."

"He's alive." Becky rose to her feet. "Cindy survived as well, but she's got to get medical attention. I don't know where Melanie is."

Adam got up and rushed through the trees to Mike. Becky watched him rouse the old man and then hug him as she made her way over.

Mike looked like he was dazed easing back from Adam's arms. "I thought I was having a heart attack. My chest was tight and I couldn't breathe."

Adam held him by the shoulders, looking him up and down. "Angina attack. Probably brought on by the stress last night."

Mike nodded, holding Adam's eyes. "Did you break that damn thing?"

"It took everything I had, but yeah, I did." Adam looked over at Becky, "The evil entity who controls this portal showed up. I didn't think I'd be able to get past it but... I had help. I was blinded, and even my sixth sense was muddled—the power in this place was so strong.

But your friend, Dara showed up to help me. She held him off long enough for me to smash that stone."

Becky's eyes were wide listening to him, but she knew he was probably right. Look at what had happened to the rest of them, and they didn't even know what shape Melanie was in. "I think you're right. She also helped Cindy. There's no way she could have gotten off that branch that stabbed her. And I was out cold."

"Hey! Anyone want to give me a hand? Becky?"

At Cindy's shout Becky left the two men to help her friend. She squatted down and lifted Cindy's arm so that it draped over her shoulders. But Cindy was heavy and there was no way she could get her up and walking on her own. "Adam! We've got to get her to the hospital. Help me."

Cindy tugged at Becky's arm. "They're alive? Did they do it?" Her eyes were clear staring at Becky, her pain forgotten.

"Yes. Adam did it. Mike had some kind of angina attack or something."

Cindy yanked at Becky with her good arm. "*Where's Mel?*"

Adam appeared on Cindy's other side and put his arm around her waist. "Keep that arm down. We'll try not to jostle you too much so that you won't start bleeding again." He paused for a moment, staring at Cindy. "She helped you too. Dara was the one who got you off that branch. She also made it cold around you to slow the bleeding. If not for her, you wouldn't have made it through the night."

"How do you know that?" Becky asked. "You were out cold too."

Adam nodded slowly. "I just do, okay?"

Becky's chest tightened, knowing that somehow Dara had helped them get through this night of terror. She was glad she'd stayed even though her head pounded like a piston. These were her friends. But what had happened to Mel?

"Ready?" Adam nodded at Becky, and together they managed to get Cindy up and on her feet.

Mike stood off to the side watching them. "Wish I could be more help here."

Adam grunted. "Just look after yourself. We've got this."

It seemed to take forever for them to thread through the path, with both Adam and Becky pushing their legs and feet through the dense undergrowth. Becky was winded, and her shoulder ached from Cindy's weight, not to mention how her head throbbed. When the forest thinned a bit and she could see the back of the resort, she breathed a sigh of relief.

But still no sign of Melanie.

Mike had been walking ahead of them. He turned his head, speaking to the group, "There's no phones to call for help, and my car's about half a mile away. Adam, either you or I will have to walk out to get it." He looked at Cindy. "We shouldn't make her move any more than we have to."

Adam looked tired but otherwise he wasn't injured. He answered Mike, "I'll go. I'm faster. I'll help get Cindy settled inside and then I'll make a run for it."

But Becky was still wondering about Melanie. Cindy, aside from wincing in pain and moaning looked like she would be okay. As for herself, there'd be a goose egg on her head but it would heal. Oh God, Melanie. What had she suffered? "I hope Melanie's okay."

Adam eased forward looking past Cindy to answer her, "Yeah. I yelled out to her last night to go for help but..." He sighed. "That place messed with my head. I couldn't even sense her anywhere in the woods after Cindy got hurt."

That could be a good thing. Maybe she'd run back from the forest. She'd stayed on the path rather than follow them to that damn altar. She may have been frightened enough to actually leave. Hell, she couldn't blame her. She'd almost left too.

The flagstone patio was just up ahead. Mike was the first one to make it there. He walked across the patio when the door to the kitchen opened.

Melanie stood in the opening, a gun in her hand.

Chapter THIRTY-FOUR

"HANG ON."

Becky didn't need to hear Adam's command. She stood rooted to the spot, gaping at Melanie in the doorway. What the hell was wrong with her pointing Cindy's gun at them? "Melanie? It's just us, for Pete's sake. Get over here and help us with Cindy."

"Put that gun down, Melanie, before you accidentally kill us." Cindy made a move forward, but Adam and Becky stood still.

"That's not Melanie. Not anymore." Adam's voice was just above a low whisper.

Becky looked over at him and was shocked to see the wide-eyed look of horror on his face. "What? Of course, it's Melanie."

"He's right." It was Melanie's voice but—deeper.

Her gaze shot to Melanie. There was a sneer on Melanie's lips, and coldness in her eyes. She stepped out of the doorway and still keeping the gun leveled, she went to the far side of the patio. "Get inside. Hurry. You first, old man."

"Look lady, there's no call for this. We were going inside anyway. We wanted to make sure you were all right. What the—"

"Shut up and move!" She pointed the gun at Mike.

Becky couldn't believe what she was seeing. They'd barely survived the night and now Melanie was threatening them? What happened?

Mike shook his head, muttering a few curses as he walked into the kitchen.

"Melanie? Why are you doing this? Cindy needs medical attention! Did you know she was stabbed?" Becky glared at Melanie, only to see her friend's expression grow harder still.

"I was there! I saw it all. She got what she deserved. So did you. Too bad the branches hadn't killed both of you. Now move. Inside!" Melanie edged closer, and her hand jerked the gun sideways signaling to the door.

But Adam wasn't moving. Instead, he glared at Melanie. "We broke the altar but it wasn't enough, was it? You're still here. You've taken over this woman."

"Huh! You're not as dumb as you look. You thought you could defeat me. You may be stronger than Dara but you're just as foolish. Now move, or I swear I'll put a bullet in both those women." She aimed the gun at Cindy.

"No! We'll go inside. Don't hurt us." Becky started moving forward, and Cindy was actually bearing more of her own weight in her attempt to get away from Melanie and the gun.

"Why do you want us inside? You're going to kill us anyway. What difference does it make if it's outside here or there?" Adam stood his ground, letting Becky and Cindy slip from his grasp.

"I should think it would be obvious to someone like you. You know I'm going to burn this place. It's going to be a terrible accident and fire that kills you all." Her gaze wandered over them. "Well...almost all. This one"—she patted her chest—"will miraculously survive. I'll also be the one who'll collect the full thirty million. That's more than sufficient to rebuild it. I'll restore this resort to what it once was. What I enjoyed long ago. Except this time, it'll be better." Melanie's eyes glittered, and there was a wet smile on her lips. She even looked taller, more alive than before.

"Not going to happen." Adam folded his arms across his chest. "You won't be able to explain the fire. Not after all the rain we've had for the last few days. And fire inspectors are better than you think."

Becky looked over her shoulder watching the exchange between Adam and Melanie or the thing that now called itself Melanie. Possession? She'd never believed in that kind of thing. But what else could it be? And in this place, anything was possible.

Becky mumbled, "We always loved you, Mel. Why would you want to kill us? You can have my share, just let us go."

Melanie kept the gun pointed at Adam but her gaze flitted over to stare at Becky, "Thanks, but I don't need your permission. And by the way, you'll soon be with your precious Dara. She tried to fight me again last night, but once more she failed."

Staring now at Adam, Melanie continued, "That stone you destroyed...it came from Turin."

"Turin...as in The Shroud of Turin?"

The Melanie-thing nodded. "Yes. There are many mystical aspects to that part of the world. We had been there for thousands of years! But we needed to leave when Europe began to burn in World War II. Generations ago we arranged for it to be shipped here at incredible expense." She tilted her head. "But it can be replaced. The power is here." Her hand swept the air, indicating the resort itself. "This so-called resort was excellent camouflage. A simple spell, and the mundane guests never saw our gathering spot. And when we needed to all gather for our rituals every equinox, we had comfortable accommodations!" Melanie's chuckle sounded like a growl.

"Why was this place abandoned, then?"

"We had to. Our camouflage stopped coming, you fool. I remained as caretaker, and the property remained in the Zuckerman family," Melanie spat. "Then that fool, Saul, whelped a daughter not a son! We needed a male heir to take over, and his bitch wife only had the one child before killing herself!"

Becky's eyes went wide. "Dara's mother *knew?*"

Melanie-thing scoffed. "She did not. She got nosy about the property—thought Saul came up here to carry on an affair and found out." It pointed toward the lake. "She had a car accident, ran into a tree on the way here. It was simple to have Dara die here. But it was fitting, don't you think?" Melanie's face twisted into a leer, and she again wetly licked her lips. "Like mother, like daughter." She plucked at her blouse. "I didn't have a human body at the time like I do now. It's' been a long time since I took one over." She licked her lips again. "I think I'll be keeping this one for a while."

Becky could only gasp.

The Melanie-thing laughed lightly. "I'm glad you didn't leave last night. This is a more fitting end for your silly gathering."

Becky saw the door slowly open wider behind Melanie. Mike stood there, a small revolver in his hand.

Melanie must have somehow sensed his presence. Quick as a cat she spun around and pulled the trigger.

And missed, the bullet splintering into the door.

She yanked at the gun, but an unseen force kept it pointed away and began to force her hand straight up into the air. The pistol fired over and over until the slide locked back, all the bullets spent.

The next moment Melanie was lifted in the air, flying backward and smashing onto the stone patio. Melanie hissed and spat at them, railing in a foreign language. Her face was twisted with rage, scrambling backward across the rough stone.

"Stop!" Adam grappled at her, but she kicked his legs out from under him. He rolled over on top of her, and she snapped her jaws at his face, then at his hands, her teeth clacking in the air.

Mike joined him, lowering to push Melanie down. With a quick move of his arms he flipped her so that her cheek was pressed into the stone. Mike scooped some kind of plastic strip from his pocket and grunted as he held her wrists together to secure them. All the while her legs thrashed but he was nimble enough to stay out of range.

Becky left Cindy's side and drifted slowly over to where Melanie was splayed on the stones. Her eyes even rolled back in her head as she continued railing out a slew of profanity. Melanie, being petite and frail had proved no match for the beefy former detective.

"What now? What's going to happen to her?" Becky turned to see Cindy struggling trying to make her way to their friend on the ground.

Adam handed the gun to Becky. "Here. I've got to go get some help here. Your friend will be okay. But watch her closely. Mike, I'm counting on you."

Becky recoiled at the deadly object in her hand. But watching Melanie was even worse. "Can you help her, Adam?"

He snorted. "I'm a psychic not a priest. That's the kind of help she needs, I'm afraid." With that, he took off, rounding the resort and was soon out of sight.

She looked at Mike. "Thank God you two were here." She looked back at Melanie. "Can she be helped, really? What happened to her? How could this thing take hold of her?"

Cindy was now next to her gazing down at Melanie. "I think she was too interested in this supernatural stuff. She opened herself to it." Tears flowed from her eyes, and her voice broke when she continued, "Melanie. We still love you. Come back to us."

For just a fraction of a second, Melanie's eyes cleared and the stream of obscenity stopped. She rolled over so that she faced them. The locks of hair that had been plastered to her cheeks were brushed back, almost like someone had caressed her cheek. A small smile curled her lips and her eyes closed. "Dara."

And in a flash, it was gone. Rage overcame her again and the litany of curses continued.

"You two go inside. Cindy should sit down and have some water. I'll look after this one." Mike looked over at Becky and then resumed his watch over Melanie.

"What are you, nuts?" Becky and Cindy said together. "We're not going anywhere!"

Cindy rubbed her wound. "Some reunion, huh?" Her head turned, taking in all of the resort. "Do you think Dara is free now? Even though that thing inside Mel said breaking the altar was nothing."

Becky sighed. "I don't believe that thing. I believe Dara. She's free, but I think she's always going to be with us." She couldn't believe she was actually saying this. She wasn't the same person as the one who'd arrived at the resort two days earlier. But she knew in her heart that Dara was watching over them.

Melanie continued to howl with white rage, sending a chill down her spine.

Epilogue...

One year later...

BECKY HAD JUST FINISHED SETTING OUT HER TOILETRIES on the bath's marble countertop when there were a few light taps on the door to her suite. She smiled, rushing from the room. It had to be Cindy and right on time too.

She opened the door and let out a squeal of delight seeing Cindy. "You're here!"

Cindy stepped closer and folded Becky into a warm hug. "Of course. Like I'd ever miss our annual reunion." She eased back, and her gaze took in Becky from head to toe. "You cut your hair. Did you lose weight too? You look different."

Becky couldn't believe that Cindy was actually commenting on it. "You're one to talk! I never thought I'd see you without spiked heels or designer clothes. Yet here you are, no makeup, wearing jeans and a cotton blouse, and you look fabulous! Come in!" She stood back and watched Cindy walk into the posh hotel room. She'd even shed the weight she must have put on during her pregnancy.

"I'm in the room next door." She looked around, taking in the posh furnishings of the living room. "Same as mine. It kind of reminds me—"

"I know. Except this place is five star, not a decrepit resort. Plus, it's on the west coast." Becky's smile fell thinking of what they'd gone through the previous year. "Do you think Mel will come?"

"I don't know. I saw her a couple of months ago. She's better but she's not the same, if you know what I mean. She's tougher, more cynical." Cindy watched Becky pour wine into a glass but raised her hand when Becky was about to pour a second. "No. I'm still breast-feeding."

"Juice?" Becky opened a bottle of orange juice and poured it in a glass. "I never thought I'd see the day that you actually settled down. The farm in Oregon, a baby, and Erik. You're a regular housefrau."

Cindy snorted. "Not quite. I run the farm while Erik writes. He also does his share of looking after Dara." She took a long sip of juice looking over the rim of the glass at Becky.

"It's sweet that you named her Dara. You must have some pics. Show me!" She forced a gaiety in her voice, but the memory of Dara hung between them like a presence.

At the tap on the door, Becky's eyes widened. It had to be Mel. She'd come to join them after all. "Hang on. I'm dying to see your precious baby, but I'm sure Mel will too!" With that she raced to the door.

When she opened it, Melanie was there, a look of wariness in her eyes. "Melanie! Come in. I'm so glad you came." She grabbed Mel's hand and pulled her inside.

She didn't say it, but she saw immediately what Cindy had mentioned. Mel was still the wispy petite blond, but there was a hardness in her gaze that had never been there before. She looked like a thin alley cat that wasn't going to put up with anything.

The steady, appraising gaze she had as she looked at both Becky and Cindy was new. It gave Becky pause. Had she really been liberated from that evil monster that had possessed her that night? Even though Adam said she was, was she *really*?

Melanie and Cindy watched each other carefully until Cindy said, "It's good you came, Mel," in a...well, maternal nurturing tone.

Melanie blinked twice, and replied, "I wasn't going to initially, but I changed my mind at the last minute." She looked Cindy up and down. "Wow! You had the baby and you look downright skinny. Well, not skinny but definitely fit."

Cindy smiled. "I named her Dara, Melanie. I was just about to show Becks some pics of her." She thrust her cell phone out, and Melanie jerked backward a bit at the sudden movement.

'Still skittish a bit,' Becky thought. She put a hand on Mel's shoulder. "Yes, let's see her!" She turned to Mel. "Can I get you a drink?" The tension in Melanie's shoulders felt like body armor.

Melanie nodded. "Jack Daniels if you have it. Otherwise, scotch neat." She stepped over to Cindy and took the phone. Looking at the screen her face brightened. "Oh my God. She's beautiful." Her voice became soft. "Dark curls, and she even has Dara's smile."

Cindy looked uncomfortable for a moment before she countered, "Erik has dark curls. That's where she gets it. But yeah, there are times when I see an expression on her face and I think of Dara."

Becky handed the drink to Mel and bent closer, examining the chubby little face of Cindy's daughter. She was adorable. She even had an olive complexion like Dara. Her eyes were drawn to a small luminescent ball of light in the background hovering over the baby. It looked as light as a soap bubble, but not transparent. An orb?

Since that experience in the resort the year before, she'd made a study of the supernatural to the point where she had become a bit of an expert on it. Even Adam thought so. She knew what that orb portended, but held her peace for now.

Cindy's finger brushed the screen bringing up the next photo in the series of the baby. Becky's fingers tightened on her glass of wine. That same orb was there...and in the next, and the next.

Melanie stepped back and walked over to the large window. "Your baby is cute, Cindy. No question. I'm happy for you." Despite her effort at sounding light, Becky heard the strain.

Becky couldn't stop herself from pointing at the orb that was in the latest photo. "Cindy? Do you see that small sphere of light in the photo? Is that in every picture you take of little Dara?"

"What? What 'sphere'?" She turned the phone and stared at the picture. Her eyebrows furrowed. "No. I've never seen that before. I would have noticed. What the hell?" She rubbed her finger on the screen to see if there was a smudge causing it. Her eyes were wide when she looked at Becky. "That's never been there before, believe me."

"Shit! This was a mistake coming here!" Melanie set her drink on the coffee table with a thud. "I'm leaving. I just manage to get back on my feet and then this. I don't need this shit screwing me up anymore."

Becky stepped over to Melanie blocking her path as she was about to leave. "No Mel. Please. Stay. Look, we'll go for a walk. We wanted to cruise through our old alma mater. Let's get out of here and get some fresh air."

Cindy slipped her phone into her cloth slouch bag. "Fer sure! I don't want you to leave. Stay so we can at least have dinner together. Then if you need to go, go." Her face was ready to crumple in disappointment. Again, in her newly found gentle voice, she added, "Please Mel."

Melanie watched Cindy and then slowly nodded. "Just a walk and then dinner. I don't think I can stay in a hotel with you guys. Not yet. It's—"

"We know." Becky put her arm over Mel's shoulders. "We'll see the sights and talk about what's happening in our lives now." She let out a sharp laugh. "You'll never guess who my ex has taken up with."

Cindy followed Becky's lead, changing the subject. "Who? Wait. Let me guess. That skank Rachel Moore. I heard she moved to Seattle."

Melanie mumbled, "Didn't he date her before you?"

Cindy caught Becky's eye, raising her eyebrows. Becky continued the Hank harangue; she could recite it by rote. Inwardly she breathed a small sigh of relief. Melanie would stay for a little while at least, if they could manage to keep the conversation on anything but Dara or her resort. It was still too fresh and painful on Mel. After all, of the three of them she had paid the highest price.

***

Over dinner they laughed until their sides hurt when they each confessed to giving Mike and Adam a reward of a million dollars apiece without telling one another. None of them wanted the other women to feel any pressure, so just went and did it themselves.

"What's friendship mean if you can't sneak a mil here and there?" Cindy cracked.

Even Melanie lightened up a little, snorting, "I did some other sneaking myself."

"Oh?" Cindy said. She leaned forward. "A little hubba-hubba on the psych ward?"

Becky almost started crying with relief when she saw Melanie take a playful swat at Cindy.

"No, momma-bear," Mel said. "No risqué stories for you on that score. I *did* however sneak away from the hospital."

"Where did you go?"

"Over to Saranac Lake where Adam and Leah are from." She took a sip of her drink. "In fact, it was Adam who busted me out..." She shrugged. "I mean, I was there voluntarily and all, so we didn't have to scale walls and stuff, but I did leave without telling anyone on staff I was going." She downed her drink and put it on the table. She looked at her two friends. "And I never went back."

"You were never discharged?" Becky asked. Uh-oh...

"Nope." She shook her head. "Didn't need to. I'm okay."

"You're different, Mel," Cindy said.

Melanie looked at her, a slow, knowing smile spreading over her face. "Are you the same after having a baby?" She turned to Becky. "And you after having your marriage break up?" She shook her head. "Of course, I'm different! We all are after that weekend."

"You're harder, Mel-a-girl," Cindy whispered. "You're like a..."

"An ex-convict or something?" Melanie laughed softly. "My firefighter says that nowadays." She put her hand over Cindy's. "I'm not *harder* Cyn-dee-girl... I'm a damn sight stronger, that's all." Her eyes flitted to both of them. "It was Adam's girlfriend Leah that saw the difference." She snorted. "And she didn't know the shrinking violet I was before. But she saw how I was struggling to become strong." She took a deep breath. "In fact, it was Leah that helped me over that last hurdle that the hospital couldn't help with."

"What is she, a shrink like Becks?" Cindy said.

"Nope." Mel turned to Becky. "She's not a professional. She's a nineteen-year-old kid trying to figure out what she wants to do with her life."

"Well, that's some resume," Cindy teased.

Becky leaned forward. "She had the same thing happen to her that happened to you, right Melanie? A demon of some kind possessed her, right?"

"Damn you're smart, Becks," Mel replied, shooting out a thumbs up.

"*What*!" Cindy hissed. "Are you shitting me?" She looked from Mel to Becks and back. "What happened to her?"

Melanie stared at Cindy in silence until Becky said gently. "Has any of us told *anyone* what really happened at Gabbinger's Reach?" She cocked an eyebrow at Cindy. "Even your husband?"

"What? Are you kidding me? He'd have *me* committed!" She shot a look at Melanie. "No offense."

Melanie giggled. "None taken."

"That's what I mean," Becky said. "It's our story...I don't think Leah's story...what she told Mel is for Mel to tell." She tipped her head to her friend. "Am I right?"

"Yes...but I'll tell you what happened between us." Mel's face softened. She clasped her hands on the table top. "When...that thing took me over...I hated you both with such...ferocity." She kept her head down, staring at her hands. "Before you guys say anything, you need to understand just how insidious it was when it was in me. I didn't feel it inside...I just felt such a deep, raging hatred for you both." She let out a long sigh. "And even after Adam and the people helping me were able to banish it, it left behind..." she shrugged. "Leah says they're 'scars on your soul', and she's right."

A single tear began to course its way down Melanie's cheek. Becky and Cindy watched it barely breathing, let alone move.

"I didn't want to kill you guys or anything after that thing left me..." Her lips formed a tense frown. "But...I didn't *like you guys no morrre...*"

Becky heard a soft gasp from Cindy, but both women remained silent. This was Melanie's story to tell.

"Those scars of the soul run deep, guys," she said. "After a while you get used to them or something. But...I knew they weren't...right? True? I mean, I knew they were keeping me from getting all the way better, but I didn't know how to fix it!"

Her hands left the table top to cover her face. Her shoulders began to tremble as she sobbed into them. Through her hands, the rest of it rushed out.

"It was Leah who showed me! Silly Leah! She's as fascinated with the occult as I used to be! Maybe even more so, because she's got absolutely no paranormal gifts!

"She told me she felt the same way towards her family, and to Adam—who she had just met!—she *didn't like those who loved her* just like me! And...and then she figured it out!"

"What happened, hon?" Cindy asked softly.

Melanie dropped her hands and wiped her face with the table napkin. "She said she didn't like any of the people who loved her, and then it dawned on her, and she asked me the same question she asked herself!"

"What was it, Mel," Becky said, egging her on.

"She said, she knew I didn't like you guys no more...but then she asked, "Who did I love?" She dropped the napkin, and turned to the others, reaching out to Cindy and Becky with her hand. "And I said right away I loved you guys!"

Cindy grasped Mel's hand tightly. "You always did, Melanie-girl. You always did!"

Becky grasped the other hand. "Yes! You always did!"

"And...and..." the tears were flowing freely from Mel's eyes now, as the three of them all began to cry. "And... just like that, the scars got better." She shook her head. "Just. Like. That!"

The three of them huddled together at the table, holding each other in love and gratitude.

"You sure know how to throw one hell of a girls' night out, Becks," Cindy quipped through her tears.

***

It was shortly after that they returned to the hotel.

Becky turned to Melanie as they rode the elevator to the sixth floor. "Are you sure you won't stay the night? It'd be nice to meet for breakfast and then sightsee some more. I don't see either of you guys enough."

Melanie was silent for a few beats before she spoke. "Well, it is late. I'd probably have three hours waiting at the airport for the next flight. I suppose—"

"Great!" Cindy grinned at Mel. "I haven't been in a big city for too long. I'd like to do some shopping."

Becky nudged Cindy with her shoulder. "You can take the girl from the city but you can't take the city from the girl."

"Count me out on shopping. But I'd like to visit the library and maybe a museum." Melanie was even warming up to the idea of staying and spending time with them.

Becky grinned. "It's not that late yet. Come to my room for a nightcap. I want to hear more about this guy you've been seeing, Mel. Sounds like it could be serious."

Melanie's cheeks flushed, and there was a small smile on her lips. "Yeah. The fireman. It's not just once a month anymore with Cody. He asked me to move in with him. I don't know though."

The elevator doors slid open. "Let's go," Becky said, "cuz I need to *go*." Their footsteps were drowned in the plush carpeting walking to Becky's room. "Live a little, Mel. He sounds nice. But try it out for size before you jump into marriage or anything." She opened the door and led the way inside, flipping the lights on.

Cindy stopped short in the hallway. "Why us? Why them?"

The others stopped, looking at her in confusion.

"What do you mean, Cindy?" Becky asked. She needed to use the washroom, but the look on Cindy's face concerned her.

"I mean...the three of us had a thing with Dara, and demons or whatever you want to call them. As luck would have it, Dara's lawyer *just happened to know* exactly the right people to call to help us."

Melanie bit her lip. "I want to say just lucky, but..."

"Yeah. But. And then you find out that Leah had just gotten to know Adam before things went ka-blooey, right?"

Melanie nodded. "And just before that, there was other stuff..." She looked over to Becky. "It's like links in a chain or something."

Cindy nodded sharply. "Yeah! Something like that! We never would have met Adam and Mike..."

"Unless Adam knew Mr. Wilson the lawyer..."

"And Leah."

"Who knew Jake..."

"Who's Jake?" Becky asked, hopping on one foot. "Look, can we finish this in the room? I gotta go..."

"Yeah, sure," Cindy said. "It's just weird, you know?" she added as the three of them entered the spacious room.

"It just got weirder!" Cindy said. Her hand shot up and her fingers dug into Becky's arm. Becky turned to face her, but the look of astonishment on Cindy's face staring across the room made her turn to see.

Oh my God. There on the small coffee table next to their empty glasses was a sprig of jasmine, a yellow rose and a bunch of lilacs. This time it wasn't Melanie insisting it had been left by Dara. It was a fact that all of them knew.

Melanie was the first to break the silence that stretched and reverberated like a piano note. "She's here."

Becky took Melanie's hand, squeezing it. "She never left us, Mel."

Cindy slipped her cell phone out and turned it to the photos of her daughter. "She's with us every day. And showing up in these photos only when we met for our annual reunion proves it."

Melanie edged back closer to the door, but Becky tightened her grip on her hand preventing her from going out. She looked at Mel. "She loves us, Mel. Loves you. What happened to you at that resort is over. The place burned down. The police said it was the work of vandals but I've got another theory. I think Adam and Mike did it. You're free of the bad things that attacked you there. But you'll never be free of Dara and her love for you."

Tears filled Melanie's eyes and she slouched lower. "I know." She looked up, staring into Becky's eyes. "I *am* all better, right?"

Becky nodded. "After those two priests worked day and night on you for days, then the doctors at the hospital...then meeting Leah... Yes, you're all better. That *thing* is gone." She gestured at the flowers spread before them. "But Dara isn't."

The three of them looked at each other silently for a moment or so. Cindy smiled. "I'm glad she isn't. Even if we just feel her more strongly when the three of us get together, I'm glad for that."

Becky wasn't even remotely close to being the skeptic that she'd been a year ago. It felt good, even if it was scary at times delving into the paranormal. She pulled Cindy and Mel to her and they hugged. "I'm glad too."

The END

Author's Note:

About 'The Haunted Ones'

I hope you enjoyed 'The Haunted Gathering'. For me, this has become my most enjoyable book I've written to date. It's also the fourth novel in my series The Haunted Ones.

The Haunted Ones are tales of ordinary people who encounter spirits from the beyond. Often these spirits are evil in nature, but other times they're spirits pleading for help. When I began these books, I originally intended for them to be complete stand-alone novels; a collection of independent tales.

But the best laid plans of mice, men and Michelle's often go awry!

My problem was that I just wasn't ready to let go of some of the characters when I finished the novel. Lo and behold, as I would write the next one, the character I missed the most would pop up and fit so well into the current work!

In The Haunted Gathering, you met Adam and Mike. Their own tale of confronting entities from beyond is told in the previous book, 'Haunted By The Succubus'.

Below is a listing of each tale of 'The Haunted Ones'. I hope you enjoy them as much as I have!

The series begins with The Haunted Hideout.

The first book is **'The Haunted Hideout'**, which came to me when I had the thought "What if an FBI safe house turned out to be haunted?"

The second book is '**A Grave Conjuring**'.

Two young sisters, wracked by guilt over their parents' sudden and tragic death try to reach out to them. But when they open the door, other, spirits come through. Spirits that are enraged.

The third book is **'Haunted By The Succubus'**. It's Adam Rafferty's story. He's gifted in the paranormal, but untrained. His youth and naiveté, combined with his gifts bring his world crashing down. If you enjoyed 'Odd Thomas' books, you'll find this tale worthwhile.

The Fourth book is **The Haunted Reckoning.**

She's haunted by the ghost of a little girl. A strange web of horror binds them. Only truth will set them free.

The Sixth book is **Graveyard Shift**.

A portal of evil has opened in the rest home. The fierce rivalry of the two nurses is a weapon to be used. All hell breaks one fated night.

The Haunted Ghost Tour is the Seventh and Final book in the Haunted Ones series.

Excited to begin his new job as a tour guide in a Haunted Walk of his city, Ryan isn't prepared for what happens. Ghosts are real, not just an entertaining tale. And they've noticed him. They're coming for him.